D1198986

ARMED
AND DISARMING

Other books by Rosemarie Naramore:

Just in Time

ARMED
AND DISARMING

•

Rosemarie
Naramore

AVALON BOOKS
NEW YORK

© Copyright 2009 by Rosemarie Naramore
All rights reserved.
All the characters in the book are fictitious,
and any resemblance to actual persons,
living or dead, is purely coincidental.
Published by Thomas Bouregy & Co., Inc.
160 Madison Avenue, New York, NY 10016

Library of Congress Cataloging-in-Publication Data

Naramore, Rosemarie.
  Armed and disarming / Rosemarie Naramore.
      p. cm.
   ISBN 978-0-8034-9952-2
   1. Policewomen—Fiction.   2. School principals—Fiction.
I. Title.

   PS3614.A685A89 2009
   813'.6—dc22

                                        2008052514

PRINTED IN THE UNITED STATES OF AMERICA
ON ACID-FREE PAPER
BY HADDON CRAFTSMEN, BLOOMSBURG, PENNSYLVANIA

For Mom and Dad

Chapter One

Melody Hudson adjusted her duty belt, shooting a quick glance at the .45 caliber pistol secured in the holster at her side. Absently she patted her chest to be sure her badge was in place, hiked her bulletproof vest into a comfortable position on her torso, and then glanced down at her boots. She grimaced. Her left boot was untied, and getting it retied wouldn't be easy, considering that bending at her middle was a virtual impossibility with all her gear already on or in place.

"Put your boot up here, and I'll tie it for you," her father offered gruffly, watching her from his place at the kitchen table.

How his little girl, five feet nothing, managed to hoist around all that police gear on her tiny frame was beyond him. Frankly, Tank Hudson wished it had been

1

beyond her, literally. If only she hadn't breezed through the rigorous testing required to be a police officer. If only she hadn't had astounding strength and stamina for a person of her stature. If only she hadn't been so eager to follow in his footsteps.

"Thanks, Pop," Melody said, pulling out a chair beside her father and dropping her foot onto it with a thud. Her father quickly tied the laces for her, tapping her boot to show he'd finished.

"You're good to go," Tank said, pushing back from the table and awkwardly standing. He teetered slightly and made a grab for the back of the chair. He didn't think he'd ever get accustomed to lugging around the cast that extended from the top of his thigh all the way down to his toes.

"All right, Pop?" Melody asked with concern, reaching for his crutches and passing them to him. "Your appointment with the orthopedist is Wednesday, right?"

He nodded with a grimace. "Here's hoping they change out the cast."

"Shorten it, you mean?" Melody asked, adjusting her duty belt again.

He nodded. "I'm so darned tired of the thing."

"I know," she said soothingly. "But another couple weeks and you'll be good as new."

Tank gave his daughter a skeptical glance. "Four to six weeks, and I'll never be as good as new," he complained.

Two months before, Tank had been involved in a serious accident on his way home from his job as commander at the Trentonburg Police Department. He had been in his patrol car and had pulled over to assist a motorist whose car had broken down. As he'd approached the vehicle on foot, a drunk driver had swerved off the road and struck him, sending him careening into the air. He had badly broken his leg in several places, and the injury had required two surgeries already.

Melody had been at work when the call came over the radio. She had rushed to his side, as had several other officers. She'd been devastated to see her father lying broken on the side of the road, but the incident hadn't soured her on police work, much as her father had hoped it would. Melody remembered her father's first words to her when she arrived at the scene. "You need to get out of police work, baby."

He had often begged her to consider another line of work, but she simply wasn't interested. Besides, an accident like his could have happened to anyone. Her father could just as easily have been in civilian clothing and on the way home from the grocery store.

No, she wouldn't consider another line of work. Police work was in her blood, and she had never wanted to do anything else. Besides, she suspected that, had her father had a son, he probably wouldn't have objected to a boy's following in his footsteps. While she could understand her father's wish that she do something different with her life, she just wasn't interested. And she simply refused to apologize for that.

Police work gave her the adrenaline rush she yearned for—there was nothing as thrilling as racing down the highway, her emergency lights flashing and her sirens blaring. But it wasn't just the excitement that thrilled her; it was helping people, making a difference in the world. Besides, she was good at her job, better than most of the men she worked with. In fact, five years ago she had graduated first in her class at the police academy. It was something to be proud of.

Melody realized her father was proud of her, though he was hard-pressed to show it at times. She knew he worried about her, and she understood that. She was all he had left in the world. His wife had passed away three years before, and Melody was his only child.

Perhaps that's why she remained at home, living in a small house near the main house on her father's twenty-acre property. She had worried about him being alone before, though he was still relatively young at fifty-eight and had been in excellent health before the accident. But now, with his injury, there was no escaping the fact that he needed her even more. She had recently made the decision to move out of the small house and back into the main house with him.

She worried about him when she left him to go to work. If only he would allow her to hire a caregiver to help him during her work hours. But he simply wouldn't consider it. Stubborn. The man was as stubborn as the day was long. It was something the two had in common.

Unfortunately, with all the work to do around the

place, Melody found her off time full of chores that generally kept her busy from whenever she got home until bedtime. She was beginning to feel the fatigue.

Melody broached the subject of hiring someone to help out around the place again. "Hey, Pop, I've been thinking. Maybe *you* don't want any extra help around here, but I could sure use it. With all the chores inside and then all the work outside, I'm not sure I can handle it alone much longer."

Tank watched her speculatively, and Melody felt hopeful until he spoke. "You need a husband."

Melody gasped. "I do *not* need a husband," she said tiredly. "I was merely pointing out that we could use some help around here."

"You need a husband, and I want grandkids," he said brusquely. "You're twenty-eight, for Pete's sake. How long are you going to make me wait? I want to take my grandson fishing and have tea parties with my little granddaughter."

Melody chuckled ruefully. While the mental picture of her father, six feet five inches tall and solidly built, having a tea party alongside a dainty little girl seemed incongruous, the reality was, she and her father had often had tea parties together when she was a child. In fact, he had encouraged them, hopeful that his rough and rowdy daughter might develop more ladylike qualities and be more like her decidedly feminine mother.

Instead, Melody had followed her father around their property, typically toting toy six-guns at her sides and yanking the ribbons out of her hair as she trotted alongside him. Frankly, the writing had been on the wall then, Melody realized with chagrin.

"My leg itches," her father complained, drawing her out of her reverie.

"I'm sorry, Pop, but there's not much we can do about that."

He growled fiercely, and Melody opted to get while the getting was good. "Hey, Pop, think about the help thing, please."

"I just want out of this cast and back to work."

Melody stood on tiptoe and gave her father a kiss on his stubbled cheek. "Hey, it won't be long. Knowing you, you'll be back behind your desk at the station and giving us all grief in no time. Now, please, *please,* be careful today."

Tank snarled a response as she headed out the door and to her patrol car parked out front.

Melody climbed into her car and snatched up her radio, promptly putting herself into service. Soon she was driving along the highway toward Trentonburg, when dispatch radioed and advised she needed to head back home.

After hearing the call, Melody rolled her eyes and glanced into her rearview mirror. Since the roadway was practically devoid of cars at this early-morning hour, she did a U-turn and drove home.

She drove fast, exceeding the speed limit, and soon steered down the lane to her house. Out front, she hit the brakes and shifted into park, sending a spray of gravel behind her. She practically flew out of the car, dashing to the porch and taking the steps two at a time.

"Doggone it, Pop!" she shouted as she threw open the front door. "Where are you this time?"

"Still in the kitchen," he called.

She could hear the frustration in his voice and couldn't keep the frustration out of her own voice when reached him. "Darn it, Pop, this is getting tiresome! You're going to kill yourself!"

"It isn't exactly my idea of a good time either," he said grumpily.

Tank was sprawled across the kitchen floor, his arms and legs splayed out like a rag doll's. Melody stood over him with folded arms, noting how close his head had come to striking the sharp kitchen counter when he fell. "You know, Pop, if you'd hit your head, I could have come home and found you lying dead on the floor. And what if you hadn't had your cell phone in your pocket?"

"I always have my cell phone. I'm not a total moron," he muttered in disgust. "Besides, if I was dead on the floor, I couldn't use my phone anyway."

With a fatigued sigh, Melody assessed the situation. She needed to get him back on his feet and be back on her way to work.

"Okay, Pop, give me your hands." She reached both hands toward him. Tank first bent his knee and planted his good foot on the floor before taking Melody's hands.

With a groan, she tugged him upward, but since he was in stocking feet, the foot on his uninjured leg simply slid across the linoleum, and Melody nearly toppled headlong into the cabinet herself.

"This isn't working," Tank said.

"Ya think?" Melody snapped, stepping back and straightening and feeling a sharp, stabbing sensation in her middle back. "Pop, I think you've just managed to put me on the injured list too," she moaned, rubbing her aching back.

"Oh, honey, are you okay?" Tank asked fearfully. "I'm so sorry . . ."

She waved off his apology. "I'm hiring somebody to help out around here. Lord knows, you need the help. *We* need the help."

"But . . ."

"No buts," she said with a flash of annoyance. "This is getting ridiculous. You're going to kill yourself or me. I'm hiring a caregiver."

Tank read the frustration on her face. "We'll . . . talk about it tonight."

"Yes. Yes, we will," she said with authority in her voice. "In the meantime I'm going to need help getting you off the floor. I'm calling Ed. Again."

Melody placed a quick call to their neighbor, who happened to be her father's best friend. Ed Carter arrived at the property in record time. He stepped into the kitchen, followed by a man Melody hadn't seen for some time. Chase. Ed's son.

Melody's breath hitched in her throat. How long had it been since she'd seen Chase? Five, six years at least. While he'd been home to visit his folks on several occasions over the years, she just hadn't had occasion to see him. She remembered that, during one of his visits, she'd been at the police academy, and then, during another, she'd been away at a two-week training course.

When she'd last seen Chase was really neither here nor there to her now, she told herself. She was a grown woman, light-years beyond the time when Chase had been the object of her thirteen-year-old affection. She reddened even now, thinking of the day she had declared her love to him.

Admittedly—at least she could admit it now—he had handled the situation delicately, pointing out that their five-year age difference was simply insurmountable at that juncture in his life. Besides, he'd been about to leave for college—hence, her urgency to get a commitment from him. She had proposed marriage; he had declined. To his credit, he had managed to keep a straight face. Melody could laugh about it all now—sort of—but then . . .

Melody found herself staring at his familiar profile as he and his father towered over Tank, both men eyeing him with unconcealed amusement. She took in Chase's dark curls and dark eyes, straight nose, and strong chin. Handsome as ever, she acknowledged, remembering how his good looks had made her swoon.

Melody heard Ed chuckle. She turned away from studying Chase and glanced at his father.

"What are we going to do with you, Tank?" Ed demanded.

"You think this is funny?" Tank said incredulously.

"You any more hurt than you already were?" Ed asked.

"No."

"Then, yeah, it's funny. Especially since you seem to be making a habit of this. Frankly, my friend, it's a habit you oughta consider breaking. Otherwise, you're liable to break your other leg, or worse. You need to stop being so stubborn and use the wheelchair."

Tank growled a response, then seemed to register Chase for the first time. "Chase," he said fondly, stretching out his hand from his awkward position on the floor. "How are you, son?"

"Better than you," Chase quipped, leaning forward to shake the older man's hand. "It's good to see you, Tank." He turned to Melody and smiled. "You too, Mel."

"It's been a long time, Chase," she said.

"Too long," he said, watching her intently.

"You gonna get me up, or what?" Tank demanded, and Melody tugged her gaze away from Chase and back to her father.

She took a step toward him, deciding to intervene before they lifted him. Having him prone on the floor might just provide the leverage she needed. "Pop, we're not getting you up until you promise me you'll let me hire a caregiver—just until you get the cast off," she assured him.

"I don't need a caregiver," he growled for the umpteenth time. "Get me up!"

Chase watched the exchange between father and daughter. He studied Melody, his eyes widening both at the sight of a grown-up Melody and seeing her in uniform. Her tiny frame didn't appear sturdy enough to support all the gear she wore.

Little Melody had definitely grown up, he thought. Well, not necessarily up—she was as petite as ever— but she had matured into a beautiful woman. Her flaxen hair, pulled into a ponytail, was as sleek and shiny as ever, her blue eyes wide and heavily lashed, and those lips, full and enticing. He'd seen the promise of that beauty years before, but the age difference had been cavernous back then when he'd gone off to college and she'd barely started junior high.

Hadn't his mother mentioned to him that Melody had become a local police officer some years before? He recalled that she had, though at the time he'd still pictured the thirteen-year-old tomboy who had followed him around his folks' property, both annoying him and amusing him at times.

What had been a case of hero worship on Melody's part had turned into a crush when Melody hit puberty. The little girl had watched him, dreamy-eyed and clearly smitten, and he'd found her adoration cute—at least until his girlfriend at the time, Courtney, had visited his home one day to find herself on the receiving end of Melody's righteous indignation. Melody had seen the two kiss and hadn't liked it one bit. Chase chuckled at the memory, and Melody turned toward him.

Somehow she sensed his laughter had something to do with her, and she felt her cheeks grow warm. She shifted uncomfortably, absently resting her hand on the .45 caliber holstered at her side. Chase didn't miss the gesture, his dark eyes widening in shock. Their eyes locked then, Melody taking in Chase's startled expression. She glanced down, realizing her hand was on the gun. She jerked her hand away, meeting his now amused gaze.

"Well, is anybody gonna help me up, or am I gonna spend the day on this floor?" Tank demanded, and Melody was actually glad for the distraction. She turned her attention to her father.

"Are you going to allow me to hire a caregiver?" Melody demanded right back.

"No!"

"Then, Pop, I'm gonna draw a chalk line around you and leave you there. May as well, since you're liable to kill yourself the next time you fall."

"I agree with Melody," Ed volunteered. "You can't be left alone, Tank."

Tank didn't respond but simply shot his friend a dirty look.

"Watch it," Ed warned, "or I'll run home quick and

get my camera. I know Mary would get a charge out of showing the picture around her knitting circle."

Tank winced. The last thing he needed was Ed's wife seeing a photo of him lying helpless on the floor. She'd be over in a heartbeat, clucking and carrying on about how he needed a wife. And she'd probably find him one too. No thank you. "Just get me up!" Tank hollered.

"Will you consider allowing me to hire a caregiver?" Melody asked in measured tones.

"I'll . . . consider it." He would consider it. Of course, the answer would be no, but Melody didn't need to know that now.

"Okay, fair enough," Melody said, and she stepped forward to grasp one of his hands while Ed grasped the other. Just the action of bending caused Melody to wince, since a sharp pain pierced her midback.

"Let me take his arm," Chase said quickly, realizing Melody was about to help his father hoist her giant of a father off the floor.

Melody stepped back, reaching behind her in an attempt to rub her aching back. It was no use, since she wore the bulletproof vest. She glanced at her watch. She really needed to get to work, but as Ed and Chase settled her father on his feet, she made a quick dash to his bedroom for the wheelchair stowed there. Stowed, since he rarely used it.

She retrieved it and rolled it into the kitchen. "Sit!" she told her father.

Tank dropped into the chair, and Melody bent to hoist his good leg onto the support platform that caused the casted leg to jut out in front of him. Her back protested the exertion, and she reached for a bottle of ibuprofen on the nearby kitchen counter. She tipped two out and took them with a glass of water. Ed and Chase watched her with interest.

Tank winced. "Melody hurt her back trying to get me up before you two got here," he explained.

"Tank!" Ed scolded, moving to stand beside Melody. "You okay, Mel?" he asked. "Do you need to see a doctor?"

"I'll be fine," she assured him. "Hey, I want to thank you for the help—*again.*" She emphasized the word, shooting her father a look of daggers.

Tank had the good sense to look appropriately repentant, and Melody sincerely hoped his contrition would last.

"I'd better be going," she said. "Thanks again, Ed. You're a lifesaver." She cast Chase a quick glance. "Chase."

She strode out the front door, surprised when Chase fell into step beside her. At her patrol car, she glanced up at him, curious, surprised to find him grinning into her eyes. "Little Melody is a lawman," he chuckled.

"Law woman," she corrected, meeting his gaze and watching him expectantly. What did the man want? He simply stood there, grinning like a dope.

"Law woman," he repeated absently. "Sorry." Suddenly he gave her a bewildered look. "Hey, don't they have a height requirement at the police department?"

Melody glanced away, then back, snaring his gaze. "What is it you do these days, Chase? Certainly nothing that requires tact or diplomacy . . ."

"Hey," he objected, "I'm usually very tactful and diplomatic. And in answer to your question, I'm taking over as principal at the high school," he informed her, grinning. "I start today."

"I'm sure the students' parents will love you," she said somewhat snidely.

"Yes . . . hey, wait a minute!" He frowned. "What do you mean? You seem to be suggesting parents won't like me. Parents always like me."

Melody looked dubious. "If your question about a height requirement is indicative of your diplomacy skills, you're in trouble. I can just hear you now. 'Sorry, folks, but little Johnny is a meathead.' "

Chase chuckled. "Hey, I didn't mean to offend you, but you're . . ." He cocked his head, seeming to rake his eyes over her, from the tips of her tiny feet to the top of her head. "Tank must be beside himself with worry every time you go out the door," he said with unconcealed sympathy.

"I can handle myself," Melody said tiredly, then reached for the door handle on her patrol car.

To her surprise, Chase intercepted her hand. "Do you have a minute to talk? It's been, what? Five, six years since we last talked?"

Melody shrugged. It had been longer. They hadn't had a real conversation since he'd left for college years before. It didn't matter.

"I'm late," Melody said, pulling her hand from beneath his. She stepped into her patrol car, shooting him a look when he grasped the door, holding it open.

"Any chance we could get together later?" he asked. "It'd be nice to talk about old times."

She shook her head. "With Pop laid up and so much to do around this place, I really don't have the time," she said without apology.

A mock wounded expression crossed Chase's face. "Is that how you're going to treat the love of your life? If you'll recall, Melody, you proposed marriage to me. Admittedly, it's been several years since the offer was made, but hey, I'm back home to stay, and I'm willing to explore all possibilities."

Melody gasped. She didn't remember Chase's being so flip—or arrogant. Was he kidding, teasing her? Surely he was joking. She gave him a long-suffering look.

"Melody, we could make beautiful music together," he teased, finally stepping back to allow her to close the door.

"Never heard *that* one before," she muttered sarcastically as she backed her car around and drove off to her next call.

Chapter Two

Chase returned to Tank's kitchen and found his father and Tank engrossed in conversation. His dad was attempting to reason with Tank, asserting that Melody couldn't possibly handle everything around the property and inside the home without help—and soon.

"My Melody's a tough cookie," Tank protested. "She handles things just fine."

"She doesn't look so tough to me. Well, aside from the gun holstered at her side," Chase said, not realizing he'd spoken the words aloud until the two men glanced his way.

Ed grinned at his son. "Mel's a looker. Didn't I tell you that, son? And a fine woman, to boot."

"You told me, Dad," Chase said with a grin. In fact, since he'd returned home, both his parents seemed

17

intent on extolling Melody's virtues. He knew very well what they were up to.

Tank's face suddenly broke into a wide grin. "Chase, remember how Melody used to follow you all over the place, all cow-eyed and dopey in love? I thought she'd die of a broken heart when you went off to college."

"Too bad about the age difference," Ed murmured.

"The age difference doesn't mean a whit now," Tank pointed out. "Melody's twenty-eight, and it's high time she got married. I want grandkids." He shot Chase a glance, seeming to assess the younger man with a critical eye. "You want kids, son?"

Chase threw his head back and laughed heartily. "Not today," he answered, still chuckling.

"What the heck does that mean?" Tank demanded. "You want 'em someday, then?"

"Well, yeah, I want kids. I love kids. I'd be a sorry principal if I didn't love kids."

"That you would, son," Ed said reasonably.

"You like what you see when you look at my Melody?" Tank asked Chase.

Chase liked what he saw very much, though he wasn't exactly certain he should convey that to her father. But, in truth, he didn't really know Melody. She was no longer the child he remembered, and she hadn't seemed particularly happy earlier when he'd tried to engage her in conversation.

Teasing her from the get-go probably hadn't been the best idea, he admitted to himself. His humor had often gotten him into trouble when he was a kid. Fortunately, it seemed to come in handy now. As an educator, he found that kids responded to humor. No doubt it would serve him well as principal at the local high school. He had to concede, however, that Melody hadn't seemed impressed one bit. To borrow a word from Tank, not one *whit* impressed.

"Why don't you come on by for dinner tonight?" Tank asked Chase, apparently eager for Melody and Chase to renew their friendship. "You too, Ed. And Mary."

Chase cocked a grin. "Who's cooking? Not you, I'd guess."

"I'll . . . order takeout," Tank said.

"And who's going to pick it up?" Ed asked.

"I'll have Melody bring it with her tonight."

"I'm sure Mary wouldn't mind cooking something up, and we could join you here. Say, seven?" Ed offered.

"That sounds fine," Tank said, eyeing Chase speculatively.

Melody had just stepped into the diner to order her usual lunch of a turkey sandwich and chips, when dispatch called. There was a disturbance at the high school. Melody hurried out of the diner and to her car.

She sped to the location, wondering what awaited her there this time. She'd had countless calls from the high school lately and couldn't help wondering what was wrong with kids today. The day before she had gone to deal with a fight between two students, and the day before that she had taken a report on a car prowl, and later the same day a case of vandalism had occupied several hours. She didn't remember things being nearly so bad ten years before, when she had graduated.

Melody steered her patrol car into a parking space and hurried into the school. The receptionist, Jill, a good friend of Melody's, glanced up and smiled. "Principal Carter is expecting you." The woman smiled broadly. "Have you seen him yet, Mel?

"Who?"

"Principal Carter. The man is drop-dead gorgeous."

"Oh, yeah, I've seen him," Melody said in a bored tone. "He was my next door neighbor growing up."

"Lucky girl." Jill's eyes sparkled. "Principals didn't look like that when we were kids. If they had, I might have even gotten myself into a little trouble—to get myself sent to the principal's office."

Melody chuckled and headed for Chase's office. She had actually attended this very high school, as had Chase, though she hadn't spent a single moment in the principal's office for any sort of disciplinary situation. Chase had practically resided there.

She had been an excellent student. Unfortunately, since becoming a police officer, she spent far too many hours in the principal's office.

She arrived at Chase's office, noting that his last name was already prominently displayed on a placard affixed to the door. CARTER.

She knocked lightly and heard him call for her to enter. She stepped inside, glancing around the room. He was alone, sitting behind a desk, but he rose when she entered the room.

She watched him, curious. "What can I do for you, Chase?"

He grinned. "Uh, nothing at this point. Everything is under control. Sit, please." He gestured toward one of the two chairs adjacent to his desk.

"What do you mean, nothing?" Melody asked, confused.

"Please, sit. You've come all the way out here. We might as well make the trip worth your time."

She shook her head, eyebrows furrowed in a frown. "What?" Melody glanced around, wondering why she'd been called to an apparently false alarm. "You don't need law enforcement?"

"Did. Don't now. Sit."

"I have to get back to work," she told him, not bothering to mask the frustration in her voice.

"Have lunch with me," he said, rising from the desk and moving to stand in front of her. He glanced down at her, towering over her. Though he wasn't as tall as her father, he stood a couple of inches over six feet.

"I have to go," Melody said tiredly. "Perhaps next

time you'll wait until you're certain we're needed before you call for law enforcement." She turned to leave.

Chase restrained her with a gentle hand on her arm. "I didn't call, but that's not important. Please, Melody, have lunch with me. My treat."

Melody met his hopeful gaze. She was hungry, and he was buying. "Why not?"

Chase led her by the elbow out of his office and, to her surprise, directly into the cafeteria, where Melody was certain not a single student missed the fact that she, Officer Hudson, was about to join Principal Carter for lunch. What had Chase been thinking?

When a chorus of suggestive catcalls erupted in the congested cafeteria, Melody shot Chase a dispirited glance. He simply smiled benignly in return, which made her want to throttle him.

Melody had worked to gain the respect of the citizenry of Trentonburg—and it hadn't been easy. At barely five feet tall, she had experienced obvious skepticism about her ability to effectively conduct herself on the job. But she had showed everyone, and she wouldn't let anyone jeopardize that hard-won respect.

Melody tugged her elbow from his light grasp, and he shot her a curious glance before breaking into a wide smile. He nodded, urging her toward the line of students awaiting their prepared school lunches.

Good grief. This wasn't what she'd had in mind when she agreed to have lunch with him. But then, what had she been thinking? That they might drive off campus for lunch at a nearby restaurant? Yes, that's exactly what she had been thinking.

Melody selected a salad from the school lunch offerings, as well as a carton of chocolate milk. Chase paid their ticket, and she followed him past the curious students and into the staff lunchroom. She recognized many of the people there.

She greeted several before joining Chase at a circular table near a window. Chase shot a glance at Melody's lunch selection. "Is that really all you're having?"

She nodded, noting he had selected pizza, salad, fruit, and a cookie—topped off with two cartons of milk. He spied her chocolate milk. "I remember you always loved chocolate," he commented. "Remember how your mom always kept those double-fudge-chip cookies on hand for you?"

"She kept them on hand as much for you as me," Melody pointed out, but she couldn't help smiling at the memory of the well-stocked cookie jar in her mother's sunny kitchen.

"I was sorry to hear about your mom," Chase said. "I felt so awful, missing her . . ."

"Funeral," Melody said softly. She waved off his apology. She knew he had been out of the country when her mother passed away, so she understood his absence.

"You must miss her," Chase said sympathetically.

Melody nodded. "It's been three years, but it's still hard for me to believe she's gone."

A slightly melancholy but companionable silence ensued, but finally Chase broke the quiet. "So, you've been a cop for how long?"

"I've been a *police officer* for five years." She emphasized *police officer,* always slightly bothered when people referred to law enforcement officers as cops. It just seemed to demean the job they did.

"Five years," he repeated, shaking his head slightly.

Melody watched him, perplexed. Why was he shaking his head?

He read the question in her eyes. "You seem so delicate and feminine now," he observed. "Definitely not the tomboy you used to—" His eyes widened as he realized he'd voiced the thought aloud.

"What does that have to do with anything?" Melody asked.

He shrugged. "Oh, I don't know. Nothing, I guess. I do know Tank must worry about you a lot."

Chase had said the very same thing earlier at her house. "I worry about Pop too," she said pointedly. "Worry comes with the job, I guess, but you learn to deal with it."

"Have you ever considered another line of work?" Chase asked with interest, and then he took a bite of his pepperoni pizza.

"Why would I?"

"Oh, I don't know," he said. "Seems like an awfully dangerous line of work if you're considering marriage, children—you know, home and hearth."

"Who said I was?" Melody said, stabbing a piece of lettuce with a sharp plastic fork and cramming it into her mouth.

"You're not? Don't most women . . . ?"

"Chase Carter, that's as antiquated a notion as I've heard out of anyone's mouth in a long, long time."

Chase smiled ruefully. "Let me pull my foot out of my mouth. Look, I'm sorry. I don't mean to offend you. It's just . . ."

"What?"

"Don't you want all those things, Melody?"

He truly hadn't meant to offend her, but as he approached the age of thirty-four, he found himself wanting those things more and more.

Melody pondered the question, suddenly wishing she was anywhere but sitting across from Chase Carter at a tiny table. His good looks tended to distract her, particularly as his gaze swept over her, his eyes clearly registering pleasure at what he saw.

"I suppose I might get married someday—*someday* being the operative word," she said a bit crossly.

"Have you ever been shot at?"

The question came out of nowhere. Melody was taken aback.

"Well?" he prompted.

"A time or two," she admitted.

He tipped back in his chair, folding his well-muscled arms across his chest. He shook his head, watching her with an expression she couldn't define. The look grew thoughtful, intense, and she flushed under his speculative gaze.

"What?" she demanded.

"I've been thinking. I understand that law enforcement has responded to calls here at school on a near-daily basis. I'm hoping to change that, and to that end, I think it might be wise to install a Director of Campus Security on-site. I intend to take it up with the school board. If they go for it, you want the job?"

Melody gave him a startled glance. "You've been on the job for how long now, Chase?"

"Today," he said succinctly. "I plan to shake things up around here," he said ominously.

"And you've given this idea about an on-site campus security officer a good deal of thought?" she said with a dubious chuckle.

"Well, yeah. You want the job?"

Melody pushed back from the table, still chuckling to herself. No, she didn't want the job. She had a job—a job she loved.

"I need to get moving," she said. "It's been nice seeing you." Well, not exactly, but he'd given her a good laugh anyway. An on-site campus security officer at the high school? As if the board would even consider it! In light of a recent failed bond measure, they hardly had the money to purchase textbooks.

"You haven't finished your salad," Chase pointed out.

"I'm full, and duty calls." She snatched the chocolate

milk off the table—no sense wasting perfectly good chocolate milk—and strode out of the room.

"You can't possibly be full. . . ." She heard Chase's words trail behind her.

She hadn't realized Chase had followed her until she sensed a tapping on the back of her bulletproof vest as she opened her patrol car door. She spun around.

"Good grief," Chase said, "that thing can't be comfortable. How do you move in it?" He grimaced, shifting uneasily, as if the mere thought of wearing the constricting vest was too much to take.

"You get used to it. Is there something else you wanted, Chase?"

He leveled a suggestive gaze at her and she flushed. He chuckled, his eyes crinkling at the corners, just like they had when he was a kid. She shot him a withering glance, and he shrugged good-naturedly. She turned to go.

"How's your back?" he asked suddenly. Had she imagined it, or had she felt Chase run a gentle hand over her back? She couldn't be sure, thanks to her body armor. Just the same, she felt a flutter of awareness and swallowed a lump in her throat.

She turned back to him. "My back's fine. Fine. Is that everything?"

"For now. See you tonight," he called cheerfully. He strode off then, whistling a happy tune.

Mouth agape, Melody watched him go. What had he meant when he said he'd see her tonight?

Chapter Three

Melody signed off work after a long day and headed for home. She'd responded to more calls than she could count today. Since Trentonburg was a college town, home to a state college, Melody often responded to on-campus calls there.

When she had worked the graveyard shift, she spent countless hours at the college, dealing with rowdy weekend revelers. In fact, it was a student from the college who had driven while under the influence and struck her father two months before.

Melody grimaced at the memory. The kid had turned twenty-one the day of the accident and had begun his afternoon celebrating with friends at his fraternity house. Drinking was no longer allowed at the frat house, though Melody realized school administration couldn't easily police the goings-on at that fraternity or any of the other fraternities or sororities on or off campus.

Her father's accident was still being investigated by Traffic Homicide Investigators, who, despite their name, handled serious injury as well as fatality accidents. Melody hoped they would soon receive a report from the prosecutor's office about whether they intended to charge the kid. Melody had been startled to see the toxicology report on the boy just days before. His blood alcohol level had been .20, over twice the legal limit in the state.

Currently Melody worked the day shift and couldn't deny she missed the later shifts. Undeniably there was a good deal more excitement working both swing and graveyard. But with her father on the injured list, he needed her home evenings and nights.

Melody was later than usual tonight, having been caught up in a domestic-violence dispute that had resulted in the arrest of a woman. She had stayed on the scene to assist the swing shift before heading home. The woman at the call had slapped her husband in a fit of anger, and, as was the law, she was considered the aggressor and taken to jail. It had been a pitiful situation. It was a shame, the state of many marriages today, Melody had thought as she left.

As Melody pulled into her yard, she immediately spied Ed Carter's car parked out front. She was glad to see that her father had company. She knew Ed did what he could to keep an eye on her father and to keep him entertained while she was at work, but he had his own unending responsibilities with a farm to run.

When she stepped into the house, shedding her gear as she entered, her father called to her from the kitchen. She popped her head in, surprised to see Tank sitting with Mary, Ed, and Chase at the table. An enticing assortment of food covered the tabletop.

"Hungry, honey?" Tank asked. "Mary cooked up a delicious spread for us."

"It looks that way," Melody said, smiling at Mary.

"You go get out of those work clothes and hurry on down," Mary said affectionately.

Melody smiled, opting to ignore Chase, who watched her with a sparkle of humor in his brown eyes.

Melody secured her weapon in a gun safe and hurriedly dressed in jeans and a comfortable burgundy T-shirt, then slipped her aching feet into a pair of slippers that had seen better days. Her left big toe jutted out of the top of the slipper, but she couldn't bear the thought of parting with the well-worn footwear. She turned to leave her room but first dashed into the bathroom to check her face and hair.

There was no denying she looked tired, since dark half-circles framed her lower eyelids. She studied herself briefly, reaching up to slip her blond hair out of the clasp that held it back. She ran her fingers through it, fluffing as she went, but gave up when she didn't get the desired results. She did refresh her makeup slightly before heading downstairs. Why she cared what she looked like was beyond her. It wasn't as if she wanted to impress anyone.

Back in the kitchen, Melody took the only available chair, between Chase and her father. She slipped into the seat, attempting to avoid physical contact with Chase, who watched her from between heavily-lidded eyes. He wore a smile and it was almost as if the man had a secret she wasn't privy to.

Ed passed Melody a plate, and she smiled her thanks. She dug in, realizing she was famished, but she flamed with color when she realized that everyone was watching her devour her food.

"I don't know where she puts it," Tank said with a shrug.

Melody dropped her fork and shot her father a glance. She was hungry, for Pete's sake. She looked Chase's way, noting he watched her father with barely concealed shock.

Chase surprised her when he rallied to her defense. "Tank, I happen to know that Melody didn't have time for a proper lunch today."

"Didn't *have* time or didn't *make* time?" her father muttered, clearly dubious.

"Well, I, for one, enjoy seeing a woman with a hearty appetite," Ed commented. "I just don't know what to make of women who sit around dabbing a piece of lettuce into a tiny cup of dressing and calling it a meal. It's no way to live," he added with a shudder.

Chase smiled in Melody's direction, and she knew

he was remembering her lunchtime salad selection at the school cafeteria.

"No way to live," Ed repeated for emphasis.

"Well, it's a good thing you feel that way, dear," Mary said with a chuckle, spreading her arms wide and drawing attention to her plump frame.

"You're perfect, my dear," Ed said, and Melody could tell by the affection in his eyes and voice that he meant every word.

Melody stole a glance at Chase, and he continued to watch her as if he were trying to figure out exactly what made her tick.

When everyone had finished eating, Ed suggested that the group retire to the wide porch out front to enjoy the dessert of chocolate cream pie Mary had made. Melody perked up at the mention of the chocolate pie and was soon ensconced on the porch swing between Chase and his mother. She wasn't exactly sure how it had happened, and she shot a furtive glance at Chase.

Her father sat in his wheelchair, his cast jutting out in front of him. He seemed content in the cool evening breeze. Ed sat in a chair nearby. The group was silent for several moments, enjoying their pie.

Chase broke the silence. "You know, it was on this very porch that Melody proposed to me," he said.

Melody shot him a startled glance, and the others chuckled.

Chase took their laughter as a cue to continue. "She

begged me not to go off to college but to stay in Trentonburg and give her time to grow up. She told me Courtney just wasn't the right woman for me. Remember Courtney?" he asked his parents.

"Oh, yes. Melody was certainly right about that girl," Ed said adamantly, his head moving up and down. "Even at thirteen Melody had a maturity beyond her years."

"Too true," Mary agreed, her brown curls bobbing as she nodded vigorously. "Melody had the girl pegged, all right. Though I don't like to speak ill of anyone, I could not abide that awful, awful girl."

"Anyway"—Chase coughed and cleared his throat—"Melody told me that if I'd wait for her, she'd marry me, give me all the children I could fit into the home of my choosing, and remain a loyal and dutiful wife."

"I did not!" Melody said with a disgusted snort.

"Oh? But that's how I remember it."

"I asked you to wait for me," she said with a laugh. "I didn't promise a . . . a . . . brood of children. I was thirteen, for heaven's sake!"

"You sounded awfully sincere to me," he said with a throaty chuckle. "And, interestingly, you seem to have forgotten your promise altogether. I've certainly kept my part of the bargain."

"What are you . . . talking about?" Melody asked.

"I was saying, I've kept my part of the bargain. I've avoided any matrimonial entanglements to date. And, just so you know, I've given the original offer consideration, and I may very well take you up on it, although it's perhaps a tad too early to tell."

"Well, yes, being as you're just recently back home," Ed said reasonably. "But Melody is a dandy, son. I'll bet if the two of you spent some time together . . ."

"What a splendid idea," Mary enthused. She took hold of Melody's hand. "Melody and Chase *should* spend some time together. I have to admit," she said gleefully, "I've always harbored a secret fancy that you two might eventually get married."

Melody gently extracted her hand from the woman's grasp—she adored Mary—and turned to Chase. "As you'll recall, my love for you went unrequited," she said sweetly. "In fact, you took my heart and practically smushed it between your fingers. Besides," she added drolly, "I've hardly spoken to you in the last fifteen years."

"I'm here now," he said agreeably.

Melody took a deep breath. She knew that Chase was only teasing her, but remembering herself at thirteen caused a mortified glow to stain her cheeks. She'd followed Chase around like the lovesick adolescent she was, which had prompted her mother to sit her down and give her a reality check. There was no denying she had been a royal pain in Chase's neck.

Melody rose from her seat and smiled at Mary. "Thanks so much for the delicious dinner," she said, "but I'd better get busy around here. So much to do," she added too cheerily. She turned to Tank. "I'll get the dishes later." To her friends she called, "Be seeing you all." And she strode off toward the barn.

Melody felt a need to escape the group. She was exhausted after having worked overtime the past several days. The last thing she needed tonight was to find herself the unwilling participant in a matchmaking scheme.

At the barn, she rounded a corner in order to inspect their firewood supply, but her ears perked up when she heard her father speak her name. She pressed herself against the wooden planks of the barn and strained to hear the conversation still taking place on the porch. Lord only knew what they were talking about now.

"As I was saying, my Melody can be a bit moody," her father said. "Don't let it put you off, Chase. A good part of the time she has a mighty pleasant demeanor."

"That she does," Ed concurred. "That she does."

Good grief. Her father was talking about her as if she were a milk cow. Had her father not already broken a leg, she might very well have turned on her heel, stomped onto the porch, and broken it for him— particularly when he kept right on talking.

"Imagine, giving a .45 caliber pistol to a moody woman," Tank said in a voice tinged with horror. "It really is a wonder there aren't more female officer–involved shootings. Melody disagrees with me on that count, of course. Once, I gave her a mug for her birthday that said, 'I have PMS and a handgun,' and she didn't even smile."

"Ooh, Tank," Mary chortled, "I might not have appreciated that either."

"No?" he asked, brow furrowed in a frown. "Huh. What do you think, Chase?"

"Well," he said, stroking his chin thoughtfully, "I think you're lucky Melody didn't kneecap you back then. You'd have had it coming, my friend."

"You think?" Tank asked.

"I think," Chase said.

"Well, as I was saying, I've always found Mel to be a most responsible and even-tempered young woman," Ed said in Melody's defense. "Lord knows, she was a superb student and athlete. She sure shined in basketball. Had she been a foot or two taller, there's no telling what she could have done on a court."

Melody had just been thinking how much she appreciated Ed's coming to her defense, as he often did, but suddenly the picture of herself two feet taller caused her to erupt into peals of giggles. No doubt she would have been superb on the basketball court then—she'd have been seven feet tall!

Had Melody not been cracking up laughing, she would have heard her father and the Carters urge Chase to follow her. "Women like that," Tank said knowingly.

Chase found Melody doubled over with laughter. When Melody spied his feet, she glanced up, curious. "I've come after you," he said.

"What?" Melody said, forcing back laughter and

then straightening to her full height and taking a deep breath.

"I've come after you," he repeated. "I understand that women like that." A smile tugged at the corners of his lips.

"What?" Melody asked, puzzled but still chuckling.

Chase waved off the question. "What's so funny?" he asked, watching her with interest.

"I was just imagining myself two feet taller. . . ."

Chase shook his head but then he remembered his father's comment. "Two extra feet? That'd put you at—what?—five-two?"

Melody shot him a look of daggers.

"Hey, no need for that hostile look. I've always liked petite women."

"Well, go find yourself one."

Chase chuckled as he followed Melody into the barn, where she promptly picked up a pitchfork. She shot him a menacing glance before she turned toward a stall and began tossing hay around.

Chase watched her, curious. "Hey, Melody, you know I was teasing back on the porch, right? I didn't mean to upset you."

She sought his gaze and saw the concern in his brown eyes. "Don't worry about it."

He glanced around. "Do you still have a horse?"

"No."

"Then what's the hay for, and why are you cleaning the stall?"

"I don't know. You should probably get back to the others. I imagine they're missing you about now." She urged him off with a flutter of one hand.

"If I didn't know better, I'd think you were trying to get rid of me," Chase observed with an exaggerated wince.

Melody fixed him with a penetrating gaze but didn't bother responding.

"Well, then," Chase said, clasping his hands together, "anything I can help you with?"

"Nope. I have everything under control."

Melody propped the pitchfork against a wall and scanned the barn. Desperate to look busy, she picked up an old rusty bucket and moved it to a different location. Why? No reason, really. She groaned inwardly. She was doing unnecessary busywork outdoors when there really was work to be done indoors. She started to leave the barn.

"Where are you going?" Chase asked. Suddenly his eyes lighted on her feet. "Are those . . . slippers?" he asked with a grin. "Are you sure you should be wearing those in a barn?"

"I'm going inside now anyway," she said. "There's real work to be done inside."

As she walked past him, Chase reached out and gently took her arm.

"What is it, Chase?"

To her surprise, he tipped her face up with a gentle

finger, urging her to look at him. "Melody, did I really take your heart and smush it between my fingers all those years ago?" he asked in a low voice.

She pulled away from him. "Who cares? I was thirteen. None of it meant anything," she assured him.

"I care," he said softly, and she glanced up to meet his gaze. "I'd hate to think I really hurt you, Melody. In fact, it breaks my heart to think I might have hurt you."

Melody felt her face go warm. It was old news, ancient history, a meaningless crush on her part on an older boy who had every reason to go off and leave her. No big deal.

"Don't worry about it," she said dismissively, and she turned away from him.

Melody woke early Saturday morning. She glanced at her bedroom window, noting that sunshine filtered through the lacy curtains. She rose slowly, yawned and stretched, and then flung her legs over the side of the bed. She had so many chores to do, both inside and out, she suddenly felt overwhelmed.

She took a deep breath, endeavoring to curtail the feeling. She gave herself an impromptu pep talk, telling herself to take one thing at a time and that, in due time, she'd accomplish each and every task.

Her mother had often told her that the best way to tackle any project was to approach it in manageable bits. Forget about the entire bedroom, her mother would say, but instead tackle the dresser—one drawer at a time. Well, that's what she would do. She would tackle one thing at a time.

Melody glanced around. What should she tackle first? What would her father most want done around the place? What needed doing the most?

Melody suddenly felt a bit deflated, thinking about her father. Foremost on her mind was his safety, and she believed wholeheartedly he wasn't safe at home alone. He needed help when she was at work, and no amount of her shouldering the burden of the day-to-day chores would assure his safety when he was by himself.

If only he would consent to hiring help. If need be, she would take matters into her own hands, but she really hated to upset him. He simply wasn't accustomed to feeling helpless, and she understood his frustration. She was so much like him on that count. Several years before, she had broken her arm while on the job, and she had practically died of boredom when she was forced to work a desk job for the duration of her recovery.

Melody readied herself for her day quickly, dressing in jeans and a T-shirt. She decided to start with the outdoor chores first. Washing both her economy car and her father's one-ton truck topped her to-do list, since neither vehicle had been washed for several months.

She stepped into the kitchen and found her father

seated at the table, a newspaper spread out before him. "Pop, I need the keys to your truck," she told him.

"Why, hon?"

"I'm going to wash it."

"Why?"

"Because it's dirty."

"Honey, it can wait," he said, lowering the paper and catching her gaze.

"Nope, I need to get the vehicles washed, and then I have to clean up the debris from the big storm we had a few weeks back, and then I have to pressure-wash the back steps, since there's moss growing on them— slippery moss, which could be a real hazard for you, Pop. After that, I'll start inside."

Tank glanced around. "Honey, really, leave it all for later. I'll be back on my feet . . . someday," he said ruefully, shaking his head in frustration. "Tell you what— I'll plan on staying away from the back stairs."

Melody shook her head. "I need to keep on top of things, or else I'll never catch up again. Keys!" she demanded.

He nodded at the top drawer beside the sink. "Aren't you having breakfast?" he asked. "I'd be happy to fix you something."

"I'll get something to go," she said quickly. Envisioning her father beside a hot stove caused her to shudder. She kissed him on the cheek, grabbed a granola bar, stuffed it into her pocket, and then dashed outside.

She did a cursory search for the hose and found it rolled up beneath a shrub. She pulled it out and connected it to the faucet at the corner of the house and then hurried to drive her father's truck into position close to the hose.

She parked the truck and doused it with water before applying a sudsy coat of the wash solution. She was vigorously scrubbing when she heard a vehicle drive up. She glanced up distractedly, deciding it was probably someone to see her father, since she didn't recognize the truck. She resumed scrubbing the front right tire of her father's truck with a large sponge.

She heard the visitor's vehicle door slam, and then she heard footsteps crunching on the gravel drive. The footsteps drew closer, and she glanced up to find Chase smiling down at her. "Hello, Melody."

She slowly rose from her crouched position, finding that her muscles had stiffened and her back had knotted up again. She shifted awkwardly in order to unkink her back.

"Back's still hurting," Chase observed with a wince.

"I'm fine," Melody said dismissively. "How are you, Chase?"

She tossed the soapy sponge onto the truck's hood, wiped her hands on her jeans, and then watched him, curious.

"I'm good." He glanced at the truck. "Big job. Need any help?"

Melody shook her head. "I've got it under control. Did you come by to see Pop?"

"No, uh, actually, I came to see you."

She shot him a puzzled glance.

"I wanted to see if you might be free to join me for breakfast in town this morning."

Melody remembered the granola bar in her pocket and absently patted it. "I have breakfast covered."

What did that mean? Chase wondered, watching her with a puzzled expression on his face.

Melody noticed. "Thanks for asking, but I can't."

Having Chase show up unexpectedly was a disconcerting turn of events, and she wasn't sure she was especially happy about it. Her day was busy enough without interruptions from neighbors, albeit good-looking ones.

"Lunch, then?" he suggested hopefully.

"I'm afraid I don't have the time," she told him honestly. "I have a lot to do around here."

"Let me help. As they say, two hands are better than one, or, uh, make that, four hands are better than two." He quirked a wide grin Melody remembered from her childhood. Chase's smile had lit her world back then.

"Well?" he prompted. "It would give me something to do. Besides, I think my folks need a break from me. They haven't had me underfoot since I was eighteen, and I think they're just about ready to send me packing."

"I doubt that," Melody said with a smile. She knew very well his folks were thrilled to have him home.

"Why don't I help you out around here, and then we'll go somewhere for lunch? How about it?" His hopeful, dark eyes bore into hers.

Melody considered his offer. "Well, if you're sure . . ."

"I'm sure," he said. "Just tell me what to do."

Chapter Four

Melody surveyed the back lawn, pleased to see it was finally clear of the limbs and other debris that had littered the grass for weeks. Chase had already pressure-washed the back steps, and Melody was relieved to have that particular task done and over with. She moved to stand beside Chase, who was propping himself up on the end of a rake and surveying the grounds.

"Looks good. What next?" he said.

"You must think I'm an awful taskmaster," Melody said with a soft smile. "You've been working all morning. Aren't you tired?"

"Aren't you?"

Melody glanced off into the distance and then back at him. "I'm too tired to be tired," she admitted ruefully.

Chase watched her from between narrowed eyes,

seeming to assess her features. "Dad tells me you're working yourself to death around here. He's worried sick about you."

Melody smiled fondly at the mention of Chase's father. Ed really was her biggest fan, and she couldn't help but love him for it. He often said he considered her the daughter he'd never had, and she had always regarded him like a second father.

"Ya gotta do what ya gotta do," Melody said too brightly, dismissing his concern with a wave of her hand. "Besides, with all your help today, I definitely have a better handle on the outside chores."

"Anything else I can do for you?"

"Nope, nothing. But thanks for the offer." Melody hesitantly caught his gaze and found herself entranced by his deep brown eyes. She saw the Chase of old, the young man who had made her swoon. She pulled her gaze away.

"What are you thinking?" he asked with interest, still watching her.

Melody ignored the question and checked her watch instead. It was nearing lunchtime, and she still had several loads of laundry waiting for her inside, not to mention the vacuuming, dusting, and her least favorite chore, scrubbing the toilets. She realized she shouldn't have agreed to a lunch date.

Date! Had she agreed to a date with Chase? What was she thinking?

Chase eyed her. "You're thinking you don't have time for lunch," he said knowingly.

She grimaced. "The truth is, I have so much to do. . . ."

"You have to eat," he said with a smile.

The man had a point. "What did you have in mind?" she asked.

Chase grinned, pleased that she had apparently relented. "You decide."

She returned his grin. "Pizza. I've been hungry for Giovanni's 'All-Meat Miracle Pizza Pie' for at least a week."

"I'll go home, clean up, and pick you up, in, say, forty-five minutes?"

"Thirty minutes," Melody said, "I'm hungry." And too, the sooner lunch was over and done with, the sooner she could get back to the laundry.

Chase passed her the rake, nodded, and strode off to his truck. Melody watched his retreating figure, noting he looked awfully good in those well-worn jeans. She reddened, glad no one had been witness to her blatant appraisal of her neighbor.

Melody hurried into the house and found Tank standing beside the counter, putting dirty plates into the dishwasher. "Pop! I'll do that!"

"I want to help out," he muttered. "Can't seem to do much of anything useful . . ."

"I'll take care of the dishes later. Pop . . ."

"Yeah?" Tank said as he lowered himself into a chair.

"Chase and I are going to lunch."

"That's great!" he said enthusiastically. "I saw him helping you with the chores out back. Mighty nice of him, considering how much work he has to do around his own place."

"What do you mean, his own place? I thought he was staying with his folks."

"He is, while he's building a house not too far from here. Didn't I tell you?"

"No, you didn't mention it. Well, I have to get ready. You're sure you'll be okay? Would you like me to bring you back a pizza?"

"Pizza would be great, and I'll be fine," Tank assured her, smiling like the cat that had swallowed the canary.

Melody cast him a quizzical glance. What was going on in that head of his?

Inside the pizzeria, Melody glanced around. She'd forgotten that the restaurant featured an intimate ambiance, with flickering candles and muted lighting. She realized it probably hadn't been the best restaurant choice, and she couldn't help wondering if Chase might think there was some significance to her selection. She didn't want the man getting any ideas.

The two sat across from each other at a table featuring a checkered tablecloth. The candle centerpiece illuminated Chase's features, and Melody found herself mesmerized by the play of light over the hard planes of his face. He seemed unaware of her scrutiny, instead appearing interested in their surroundings.

"Wow, I don't remember this place," he said finally. "Is it new? Great atmosphere."

"It is new, actually, and the pizza's great," Melody said matter-of-factly. "I could do without the ambiance." She held a hand out in front of her. "You can barely see your own hand in front of your face, let alone read a menu."

Chase arched an eyebrow and then chuckled. "I can see fine. Besides, it seems kind of romantic to me—a great place for a first date."

Melody gulped loudly. Was he teasing her? Did he really think they were on a date? If so, she'd nip that assumption in the bud, and fast!

"Oh . . . well, um . . ." she stammered, "it isn't as if this is a date. . . ." *Real decisive, Hudson,* she told herself, practically rolling her eyes. *You really told him.*

"No?" Chase smiled. "This isn't a date?" His eyes sparkled with humor, and Melody wondered if he was teasing her. She couldn't be sure.

She shifted uncomfortably before picking up her napkin and arranging it on her lap. "I mean, we're just . . ."

"What are we, Melody?" he asked with interest, leaning forward and watching her with a ghost of a smile on his face.

"We're . . ." She eyed him. "We're not . . . anything," she said, but then she sat in quiet contemplation for a moment or two. "We're neighbors!" she said finally, triumphantly.

Chase studied her face, then smiled, and she shifted uncomfortably under his speculative gaze. She was relieved when a waitress appeared to take their food order.

Soon, to Melody's relief, Chase began reminiscing about old times. She found herself amused by his animated recounting of his youthful adventures. Although she had been too many years younger to have taken part in any of Chase's teenage stunts, she had definitely heard about one or two of them, generally from his mother.

Mary had often showed up at Melody's house, wringing her hands and practically pulling her hair, courtesy of her mischievous son. Melody's mom, who had adored Chase, assured her dear friend that Chase would be fine, that one day he would be a responsible adult.

"Your mom and dad were on a first-name basis with Mr. Vernon, the principal, weren't they?" Melody observed.

Chase grinned ruefully. "Yeah, they used to invite him to dinner to discuss . . . me."

"I remember when he showed up at your house to talk to your folks that one time," Melody mused aloud, laughing. "I actually saw steam coming from the man's ears."

"Which time?" Chase asked with a wince. "There were too many visits to count."

"The time you colored his hair green—for some St. Patrick's Day event, if memory serves," Melody said with a chuckle.

"He wasn't amused," Chase remembered with a grimace.

"Good grief, Chase, you're a principal now. Aren't you worried about bad karma—that what goes around comes around?"

"It has crossed my mind," Chase admitted. "So you know, I have repented of my past misdeeds," he said with a smile, "if that counts for anything."

"You might want to take that up with Ol' Shark Tooth," Melody said with a grin, using the name the high school students had bestowed upon the long-suffering principal.

"Ol' Shark Tooth. Poor guy," Chase muttered. "Wonder what the kids call me behind my back."

Melody could readily imagine, suspecting that the female students had probably assigned him a much kinder and gentler nickname. At thirty-three, he was young for a principal and drop-dead gorgeous, to boot.

"Well, at least it isn't likely any of your students will be able to put anything over on you," Melody said. "You know every trick in the book."

"I invented every trick in the book," he admitted ruefully. "Heck, I wrote the book." He leaned back his chair and flashed a quick grin. "I'll plan never to fall asleep in my chair, but if I do, I will never, ever put a cap on my head without first checking it for hair dye." He chuckled. "I already make it a habit to check my chair before I sit down. I remember one time . . ." His eyes widened. "Never mind. No need for that stunt to live on in anyone's memory but mine."

"And Mr. Vernon's, I'm sure. What'd you do, Chase?" Melody prompted.

He shook his head. "You don't want to know. You really don't."

"I wonder if you'll encounter your youthful counterpart at the high school," Melody said with a mischievous chuckle. "Here's hoping he's a freshman with a wildly vivid imagination."

"Here's hoping he's not," Chase said with a shudder. "I was awful."

"You ever think about apologizing to Mr. Vernon?" Melody asked. "He still lives in town."

"Done it," Chase admitted. "He also wished a 'Chase Carter' on me. Can't really blame him, I guess."

The waitress appeared with their sodas and pizza, and Chase smiled at Melody over the expanse of pizza. "It's huge," he commented. "We'll take the leftovers to Tank."

"He's expecting it," Melody said with a smile.

After the twosome ate their fill and finally left the restaurant, Melody glanced at her watch, surprised to find they'd been in the pizzeria for nearly two hours.

The time had flown, but as much as she had enjoyed lunch with Chase, she had chores to do at home.

"That was fun," Melody told him as he led her to his truck, his hand on the small of her back.

"How about topping it off with ice cream?" he suggested.

"I can't. I really need to get home. Besides, Pop's waiting for his pizza."

"We could grab a quick cone and eat in the truck," Chase suggested.

Melody smiled. "Raspberry cheesecake swirl does sound great."

Back in his truck after a quick detour to the ice cream parlor, Melody found herself watching Chase. She suddenly remembered herself as a young teen, a girl whose fondest wish had been to go on a date with Chase.

She chuckled at the memory of her thirteen-year-old self. Funny, how personalities change, she thought. Back then, she had thought Chase was the man of her dreams—she'd truly harbored a fancy that the two of them would one day marry. Of course, she had always wanted to be a law enforcement officer too, and she had envisioned herself as a rough-and-ready cop, a crime fighter intent on ridding the world of evil. She had believed she could have it all then, but now she wondered.

Her father was so eager for her to find a husband, she was growing weary of his constant badgering. The truth was, marriage was the last thing on her mind. She realized with surprise that she hadn't dated anyone for some time, and she certainly hadn't dated anyone she considered husband material—whatever that was. Her career really had become the driving force in her life, and she knew that law enforcement was more a lifestyle than a career. Finding a spouse who understood that reality might be easier said than done, she realized.

Melody could pick out a law enforcement officer in a crowd, even if he or she wore civilian clothing. Perhaps it was an air of confidence they possessed, but Melody realized that people who entered the field were a particular breed. And she was definitely one of them.

Melody was lost to her thoughts and hadn't even registered that Chase had driven off the main roadway and down the gravel lane to her house.

"What are you thinking about?" he asked with interest as he parked the truck.

She shrugged. "My job, I guess."

"You love it."

"I do," she said with a smile. "I'm . . . good at it."

"I've heard," he told her, returning her smile. "You know, I wish you and your fellow officers weren't having to spend so much time at the high school in an official capacity—not that I don't enjoy seeing you," he added quickly. "But I hope I can find a way to calm things down around there—return the place to a peaceful learning environment rather than a veritable den of thieves."

Melody winced. She'd heard from another officer that there had been a rash of burglaries at the high school, with the thieves stealing everything from iPods to textbooks.

"Any idea who's responsible for the burglaries?" Melody asked.

Chase shook his head. "No, but I'm keeping my eyes open. I need to find a way to keep these kids engaged and out of trouble. If they're kept busy, they're less likely to become involved in other 'activities.' "

"What do you plan to do?" Melody asked with interest.

"First I need to go to the school board and implore them not to get rid of several clubs and after-school programs."

"I heard about impending cuts," Melody murmured.

He nodded. "The school board has already eliminated two of our sports programs, as well as three after-school clubs. I have to find a way to stop them. If these kids are left to their own devices, they're liable to get into all kinds of trouble. We need to steer them along a right path."

"You love your job," Melody observed with a smile.

"I do," he said. "I like kids. Maybe because I was a challenging lad myself," he admitted with a grin. "I tend to communicate with them on a level that seems to get their attention."

"You don't take any guff," Melody said succinctly, intuitively sensing it was true.

"Exactly." Chase eyed her for a couple of seconds. "I think you and I have that in common."

Melody colored under his speculative gaze, and he grinned. "But enough shop talk. Can I help you with anything else around here?"

Melody shook her head. "I've got it under control. Thanks for all your help earlier, and for lunch."

"Anytime," he said with a smile. "Really, Melody. Anytime."

Chapter Five

After Chase left, Melody turned her attention to the inside of the house. As she folded a basket of towels, she glanced at the clock above the door in the laundry room. It was nearing five, and she realized she needed to get showered and changed into her uniform.

An hour before, she'd received a call from her sergeant, advising her he needed her to pick up a short overtime shift that evening as a foot patrol officer at a carnival at a local church. She hadn't minded really, other than it meant her father would be left to his own devices for another evening.

Melody hurriedly readied herself and found her dad in the kitchen. "Are you sure you'll be all right, Pop?" she asked. "You know how to reach me if you need me."

"Ed and Mary are coming over," he told her, and she felt relief wash over her.

Melody was about to head to her patrol car but first returned to her bedroom for a pair of jeans. She remembered she had shopping to do in town and opted to drive her personal vehicle to the carnival. She had already dressed in a light T-shirt under her uniform shirt and could easily slip into civilian clothing after her shift.

Thirty minutes later, she arrived at the crowded parking lot of the church. She parked and began strolling the grounds. The carnival was larger than she'd anticipated, featuring several rides in addition to an assortment of games.

Melody recognized many carnival-goers, nodding at each as she passed. She spied a fellow officer, Chad Rowe, and approached him with a smile. "How's it going, Chad?"

"So far, so good," he remarked. "Everybody seems to be minding their p's and q's," he said with a grin. "But then, it is a church crowd."

"Glad to hear it's been quiet," Melody said with a nod as she strode off. To her surprise, she spotted Chase standing several yards away, surrounded by an animated group of high school girls. She approached and attempted to hear what the girls were so worked up about.

"But you promised, Mr. Carter," one girl accused.

"You did!" another cried.

"We told you, Mr. Carter! We did, and you said yes."

Melody watched Chase's face, which was rife with indecision. "I don't remember you asking me *this*," he said in his own defense. "It's chilly out here. You don't want me catching a cold, do you?"

"Come on, Principal Carter," a girl said persuasively. "It's for a good cause."

"Be a good sport, Mr. Carter," another girl urged.

Chase threw his hands into the air. "Okay, okay, but if I come down with pneumonia . . ."

Melody watched the group, curious, and suddenly Chase's eyes connected with hers above the crowd. He shot her a wide, rueful grin and sauntered over to her.

"You're working!" he observed with surprise. "Hey, I don't suppose you could arrest me right now?" He waved a hand toward the ever-growing crowd of girls. "They say I agreed to do a stint in the dunk tank, but I'm sure I would remember that," he said, his brow furrowed in a frown.

Melody chuckled, noting he was dressed in jeans and a polo shirt. "Come on, Chase, be a good sport," she teased, mimicking one of the girls.

"I can see you're not going to help me out of this mess," Chase said.

"Nope."

Chase glanced back at the dunk tank. "Looks cold," he observed with a grimace.

"Yes, it does. Is that what you plan to wear when you go in?" Melody asked.

"It's all I have," he told her. "Wait, no! I have shorts and a T-shirt in the truck. Walk with me?"

The two strolled across the grounds to the parking lot. Chase opened the passenger door of his truck and pulled out a gym bag. "Thank goodness I have my workout clothes," he told her.

They turned and began walking back to the carnival. Chase shot her a curious glance. "Earlier you didn't mention you were working tonight. You've had a long day."

"My sergeant called not long after you left."

"You don't get much downtime, do you, Melody?" Chase said sympathetically.

"Can't say that I do," she admitted with a smile. "But I like to be busy. Usually, anyway. I suppose I could stand being less busy these days, with Pop in his current condition."

Chase stopped walking and watched her sympathetically. "You know you can call me if you need anything. . . ."

Melody found herself warming under his gaze. "I appreciate that, Chase."

He watched her briefly. "Duty calls," he murmured, and he began walking back toward the crowd of students. Melody remained by his side, smiling widely. At the dunk tank, Chase turned to her again. "How did I get myself into this?"

"It's for a good cause," Melody said brightly, but then sobered. "What's the cause anyway?"

"The drill team is trying to earn enough money to buy new uniforms. The school board isn't willing to pay."

"That is a great cause," Melody said enthusiastically. "Besides, aren't you the same guy who wants to assure that our teens are involved in extracurricular activities? Go on now." She shooed him away. "You'd better get changed, and I'd better get to work."

"I hate it when my own words come back to haunt me," Chase said with a sigh. "Okay, then," he said without enthusiasm, but then he brightened, snaring her gaze. "Uh, Melody, what time do you get off? Maybe we could . . ."

"I won't be here long, and I have shopping to do later, and then Pop needs me. . . ."

"I understand," Chase said. "Okay, then, I'd better change."

"Okay, then."

Chase strode off, and Melody watched him, noting she wasn't the only one to stare after him.

"He's going into the dunk tank! Principal Hottie is really going in," one girl swooned. "Wonder if he'll take off his shirt."

"It's Principal Hot Bod himself," another girl said with a giggle.

Melody couldn't help but chuckle. *Principal Hottie. Principal Hot Bod.* As she'd guessed, Chase's nicknames were a long way from Principal Vernon's moniker of Ol' Shark Tooth.

Melody resumed her foot patrol of the carnival but soon found herself back at the dunk tank. Her curiosity had gotten the better of her, and she wondered how Chase was faring in the frigid water. She strolled over and noted he was seated on the platform, dressed in shorts and a T-shirt and as dry as a desert.

A boy of about sixteen approached the table where drill team members were collecting money, cheerfully paid his dollar for two attempts at the new principal, and then strutted over to his mark. He grinned at Chase, whose eyes widened with alarm. Melody noted that Chase rallied quickly, yawning as if he were bored.

"Hello, Taylor," Chase said evenly. "You wouldn't want to dunk your old principal, now, would you? Frankly, I doubt you have the arm or the aim."

"Oh, yeah. Yeah, I do," Taylor responded, narrowing his eyes menacingly. "You just watch me." The boy assumed the posture of a practiced pitcher, rearing back and throwing with power. The ball whizzed by its intended mark by only a fraction of an inch.

"Missed, Taylor!" Chase taunted. "And I thought you were a pitcher! A real pitcher!"

The boy shook off Chase's criticism, instead narrowing his eyes and rearing back with the next pitch. Missed!

The boy growled and glanced around the crowd. "Can anybody loan me a buck?"

"Are you out of cash, Taylor?" Chase called out. He

pretended to search his pockets. "Ah, shoot, I don't have any to lend you."

Taylor shot him an angry glare and pointed a finger. "Just give me a minute, Principal Carter. You're going down!"

"Promises, promises," Chase said in a bored tone.

The girls in the crowd giggled, and Melody noted that Chase looked awfully smug. She suspected he wouldn't be dry for long, and she left the crowd, resuming her patrol.

A half hour later, she returned to the dunk tank, and her eyes widened in surprise. Chase was still seated on the platform above the tank, looking bored, uncomfortable, and cold—but dry.

Melody approached a teenaged girl. "Why's he still sitting there?" she asked.

The girl grinned. "Nobody has good enough aim to dunk him. That, or he's just plain lucky. The rule is, you have to stay there until you get dunked."

"Oh!" Melody chewed her lip thoughtfully. Should she or shouldn't she? She consulted her watch, surprised to discover her shift was over. She grinned triumphantly as she pulled a wadded up bill from her pocket and strode over to pay for a chance at Chase.

Chase sat up tall when he spied her approaching the mark. "Melody, what are you doing?" he called out in mock terror. "You wouldn't dunk an old friend, now, would you?"

"If I don't, you could be there all night, Chase."

He shrugged. "You have a point. Are you off work now?"

The crowd of teenagers let out a long, collective "oooooh," and Melody was sure she saw Chase redden.

"You can't dunk me, Melody," he taunted then, getting into the spirit of things. "Many have tried, and all have failed. . . ."

Chase's words trailed off as Melody reared back and threw at her mark. She hit it dead on, and Chase dropped like a rock. He rose from the water, sputtering and watching Melody with an expression of shock and admiration. "Who taught you to throw like that?" he called out.

"Nobody taught me," she said smugly. "I was born with this arm." She tapped her biceps. "Now get back on that platform. I paid for two throws."

Chase's eyes widened. "You don't really expect me to . . ."

She nodded, gesturing with the ball. "Get up there."

With chattering teeth, Chase reset the platform, climbed back on, and then watched Melody through narrowed eyes. "If I get sick, it's on your head. . . ."

Melody reared back, released the throw, and down he went, dropping into the water a second time. To Melody's relief, he came up laughing.

"We're looking for a new pitching coach," he called, and the kids in the crowd erupted with laughter.

"Yeah, hire her," Taylor called out. "Definitely, hire *her*!"

Suddenly Melody was swallowed up by eager teens, high-fiving her and patting her on the back. She couldn't help laughing at their exuberance.

To her surprise, the crowd parted to allow Chase through. He was dripping wet, and his teeth chattered. He opened his mouth to speak, when suddenly, the boy, Taylor, sidled up to Melody.

"Hey," he said smoothly. "I was wondering how old you are, Officer, cuz you're hot. Would you like to go to prom with me?" He arched his eyebrows suggestively.

Melody bit back her laughter, and Chase dropped a muscular arm around the boy's shoulders, soaking him in the process. "Taylor," he said, "Officer Hudson is too old for you. Besides, if she goes to prom with anyone, she's going with me."

Melody was taken aback for a split second, but then she laughed. She knew Chase was teasing the boy.

"I hear ya," Taylor murmured, and he sauntered off.

Chase waved off the remaining kids. "Go, go. You got what you wanted—I'm soaking wet. You all should be happy. Go, go!"

Chase turned to Melody. "You're off work now?"

She nodded. "And you're freezing. You'd better get out of those clothes."

Chase glanced down, noting he was standing in a

puddle. He grabbed at the fabric of his shirt, pulling it away from his skin. "Brrrr," he said. "Hey, give me a minute to get dressed, and then—"

"Chase," Melody cut in with chagrin, "I really should go."

"Hey, Mom called my cell after you and I talked earlier, so I happen to know that Tank has company. Come on, Mel, stay. How long has it been since you had a night out?"

Melody considered his offer. She had to concede it had been awhile since she'd had a night out, and Chase looked so hopeful. "All right, but I need to change too. My clothes are in my car."

"I'll change first, and then I'll walk you to your car," Chase said.

"I'll be fine," Melody assured him.

"I know, but just the same, wait for me, okay?"

She relented and stood by for a moment or two, until Chase bounded out of a mens' restroom, dressed in slacks and a polo shirt once again. He followed Melody to her car, where, to his surprise, she quickly shed her uniform shirt to expose a black T-shirt, which she tugged over her head, exposing the yellow top beneath. She glanced at Chase and motioned for him to turn around. He smiled but did as he was told.

Melody unlaced her boots and tugged them off and then unfastened her pants. She stepped out of them, since she wore shorts beneath.

"Okay," Melody said, and Chase turned.

His eyes lightened on her slim, tanned legs as she reached back into the car and pulled out her jeans. He was glad she had warmer clothes with her, since there was a nip in the air. He watched her drop onto the car seat, put the jeans on, and then slip into a pair of sneakers.

"Wow," Chase said with admiration, "you have the quick change down to a science."

"Comes from my years on the job," she said.

Melody secured her gear in the trunk of her car but carefully tucked her revolver into her purse after assuring herself that the safety was on. "I can't leave my gun behind," she told him.

He nodded. "Let's head to my truck. I'll toss my wet clothes in the back, and then we can go check out the carnival," he said.

Soon the couple strode back to the festivities, Chase intent on steering clear of the dunk tank. To Melody's surprise, he took her hand, and they walked around for a half hour or so, taking in the sights. Soon, they gravitated toward the rides, cordoned off from the games by a low fence.

Melody spotted the Ferris wheel and tugged Chase over. "Let's ride," she said eagerly. "I love the Ferris wheel."

Was it her imagination, or had she seen a flash of uncertainty on Chase's handsome face? "Uh, sure . . . I'll . . . get the tickets," he said.

"I can get them. . . ."

Her words dwindled off as Chase strode toward a nearby ticket booth. He purchased the tickets, and soon they were seated on the ride together. Melody grinned as they rose higher as each new passenger or group of passengers boarded the ride. Finally they reached the top, and Melody glanced out over the crowd. She could see out over the whole carnival.

"Look, Chase, there's the dunk tank. Oh, and I see the pony rides over there."

He nodded, but she realized he didn't look at her or follow her pointed finger to the pony rides. He sat as still as a statue, his eyes fixed forward, and it wasn't until Melody began violently rocking the compartment to add a little thrill to their fun that he turned to her.

"Uh, Melody, I don't think it's a good idea for you to do that."

Melody noted he white-knuckled the rail that held them securely in their seats. She saw a bead of sweat trailing down his cheek.

"Chase," she said evenly, "you're afraid of heights, aren't you?"

He shook his head, but then the gesture morphed into an up-and-down motion. "No . . . yeah."

"Chase Carter, afraid of heights," Melody said with a low whistle. "Who would have thought?" Melody bit back a chuckle, careful to avoid any sudden movements. "Why didn't you just say so?" she asked. "I would have understood."

"Uh-huh," he said numbly, taking a deep breath.

" 'Uh-huh'? What does that mean?"

"You're an adrenaline junkie, Melody Hudson, and I'm . . . not."

"Well, you used to be," she pointed out.

"Not if it involved heights," he murmured. Chase stiffened, and Melody noted that the corded muscles in his arms went taut as he gripped the bar in front of them even tighter.

"Chase, are you all right?"

His voice was clipped when he answered. "Fine."

Melody suddenly felt awful for having suggested the ride, but he could have told her he was afraid of heights, or Ferris wheels, or careering forward and then backward at dizzying speeds.

She shot a sympathetic glance his way and realized his face had turned ashen. She bit back a laugh. It wasn't funny, so why did she feel like laughing? Chase, afraid of heights? Who would have thought?

Melody laced her arm through his and held on tightly, praying the ride would end soon for his sake. Why hadn't he simply told her he didn't want to go on the Ferris wheel?

Finally the ride slowed and then stopped altogether, and they were safely on the ground again, though Chase seemed a bit off-kilter. Melody noticed him make a grab for a post and then stand perfectly still as he attempted to steady his breathing. Finally he smiled.

"That was fun," he said with forced brightness.

"Right up there with taking a bullet in the arm," Melody said with a disgusted snort. "Why didn't you tell me you're afraid of heights?"

"I . . . I don't know," he mumbled miserably, but then he laughed. "I wanted to impress you, I guess."

"By riding on a Ferris wheel?"

"Well, yeah."

"How'd that work for ya?" she demanded in a firm tone.

"Not very well." He opened his arms wide. "I need a hug," he said ridiculously.

Melody found herself stepping into his open arms and returning his hug.

"You're warm," he murmured against her hair.

"And you're cold," Melody told him, noting his teeth were chattering again. She hoped his turn in the dunk tank, courtesy of her, wouldn't really bring on a case of pneumonia.

"Are you referring to my body temperature, my personality, or . . . ?"

Melody pulled back and shook her head. "Chase Carter, afraid of a Ferris wheel . . ." She spun on her heel and began walking away.

He fell into step beside her. "We don't have to tell anyone about this, do we?"

"No, no, of course not. May I borrow your cell?"

Chase reached for his phone, but then his eyes narrowed as he got the joke. "Funny. Hey, are you hungry?"

"How can you eat?" Melody said, incredulous. "You were awfully green not two minutes ago."

He shook his head. "The healing power of your hug."

Melody shot him a glance.

"I have a cast-iron stomach. You want to eat here or drive into town?"

Melody noted that Chase really was cold, since his teeth were chattering, but she also realized he wasn't about to admit to being cold. "Let's go into town," she suggested.

When Chase draped an arm over her shoulders, Melody wasn't sure if he wanted to be close to her or if he was simply attempting to warm up. Either way, his touch was doing odd things to her heart rate.

She sighed inwardly. The last thing she needed right now was any kind of romantic entanglement. Her first order of business was insuring that her father remained in one piece. And then there was her ongoing commitment to her job.

Her job was her life, though lately Melody had realized something that surprised her. Although she knew she would never leave law enforcement, she found herself thinking more and more about leaving the street. She had been a patrol officer for five years, and she thought she might be ready for a change within the department.

She had lasted far longer than most in the position. More often than not, officers hightailed it off patrol and into specialized units as soon as they could. Patrol meant constant activity, continuous calls, and adrenaline spiking scenarios—which, frankly, were Melody's primary reasons for loving the job for so long. But, she realized, she too was beginning to tire.

Her big fear, however, was that, should she step into a different position, she might soon grow bored, and, since entering a specialized unit meant a specific time commitment, she wouldn't be able to leave if she was miserable. She had considered joining the SWAT team, or maybe even the traffic unit as a Traffic Homicide Investigator. In that capacity, she would carry a pager and be subject to call-outs to every serious injury or fatality collision. It was a huge commitment. In truth, she most wanted a detective's position, but none was open and wouldn't be for some time.

Melody pushed thoughts of work from her mind. Why not enjoy her evening out with Chase? She could worry about work later.

Chapter Six

Melody hadn't seen Chase for nearly a week, not since spending much of the past Saturday with him. Her week had been hectic, the agenda including a trip to a nearby town to see her father's orthopedic surgeon, and then, later in the week, she'd gone out of town for two days to a training course in photo radar for the department.

By week's end she was exhausted, and she arrived home from work to find her father equally exhausted. At her father's doctor's appointment, they had both been devastated to learn Tank would be in a cast for at least two months longer, if not more. The doctor had explained that bones didn't heal as quickly as one got older.

Tank had been distraught; he hadn't said so, but

Melody could tell. She knew her father well. He'd been in a funk all week.

Tank had fallen again once during the week, though he was doing better on that front, since he relied on his wheelchair much more now than he had previously. On some level, that disturbed Melody. Her independent father had scoffed at the notion of depending on a wheelchair, had vehemently refused at one point, but had finally seemed to relent.

As Melody puttered around the house doing some light housekeeping, she was surprised to hear the doorbell ring. It was Friday night, after eight o clock, and she wondered who was dropping by so late. She strode to the door and tossed it open.

Chase stood there, looking tired but pleased to see her. "Hey, Mel."

"Hi, Chase."

He stepped past her and strode into the kitchen. She followed and watched him drop into a chair at the dinette table. He smiled up at her. "How've you been?" he asked.

"Real good," she told him, eyeing him speculatively.

"How's Tank holding up? I hear he'll be stuck in a cast longer than anticipated."

She nodded. "He's pretty blue about it too."

"I'm sorry to hear that." Chase was silent for several moments, glancing around the kitchen, apparently lost to his thoughts.

"Did you need something?" Melody prompted. "Would you like some lemonade or a soda?"

"Actually, water would be great."

Melody took a cup down from the cupboard, then filled it with ice and water from the dispenser on the fridge door. She passed the glass to him and then sat down across from him. She felt a piercing pain stab her back, and she shifted uncomfortably.

Chase noticed. "Your back is really bothering you, isn't it? Have you seen a doctor yet?"

Melody shook her head and shrugged. "It'll be better soon."

Chase lowered his glass of water. "Come here, Mel. Let me see if I can help loosen up the muscles in your back."

Melody watched him, aghast. "No, thanks just the same. I'll take an ibuprofen later and then maybe soak in a warm tub."

"Really, Mel, I can help you."

Melody shook her head. "I'll take a couple of tablets now." She rose to retrieve them, when, to her surprise, Chase reached for her hand and gently pulled her onto his lap.

She practically screamed, and he chuckled lightly. "Really, Melody, I can help ease the pain." He furrowed his brow. "It might work better if you were lying down, but we'll try it this way. Okay, relax."

Okay, relax? Yeah, right.

"Chase, my back is okay," Melody mumbled uncertainly, wondering what Chase intended to do. She gasped when he began rubbing her back. She was still sore from trying to heft her father to his feet before, and the injury had been compounded by hour upon hour of sitting in her patrol car. She suspected all the work she did around the property wasn't helping either.

She had to admit, Chase's tender ministrations were working wonders toward relaxing the tightened muscles. As Chase continued to gently rub her back, she found it more and more difficult to keep her wits about her. "Okay, Chase," she said with as much authority as she could manage, "that oughta do it."

"It feels good, doesn't it?" he said kindly. "Sit still, and we'll have you back to your old self in no time."

It felt a little too good, she admitted, but she didn't voice the thought. She attempted to slide off his lap, but he pulled her back. She found her soft curves pressed against him as he continued the gentle, delicious assault on her aching back.

"Okay, that's enough," Melody said in a singsong voice. "I'm liable to fall asleep on your lap. I'm not sure what Pop would say about that."

"I happen to know that your dad is pretty eager to see the two of us hitched," Chase said with a chuckle. "For that matter, I think my folks are practically planning the wedding."

"What?" she shrieked. "You're joking."

"There was a time *you* were pretty eager to see the two of us hitched," he pointed out with a grin. "Remember, Melody?"

"I was thirteen!"

"You were mature for your age," he teased, nuzzling her ear now.

To Melody's immense relief, Tank chose that moment to wheel himself into the kitchen. While Chase didn't immediately release her—probably since Tank was grinning from ear to ear when he found the twosome together—he did finally allow Melody to stand. Of course, her cheeks flamed when she nearly toppled over, thanks to her wobbly legs.

She rose to her full height, glaring at Chase with undisguised frustration. He met her gaze head-on, showing absolutely no remorse, and then had the audacity to chuckle when she huffed out of the room. "I was just trying to help, Melody," he said sincerely.

She bit back a retort when her fuzzy brain couldn't muster anything adequate.

"Hey, uh, I need to talk to you, Melody!" Chase called after her retreating figure.

"You had your chance!" she called back.

"Really, Melody, I need to talk to you," he said loudly. "It's about a caregiver for Tank."

"Is Melody coming back, Tank?" Chase asked hopefully, tapping his fingertips on the tabletop. "I didn't mean to scare her off. I was only trying to—"

"I know exactly what you were trying to do," Tank said with a snort.

"I was massaging her back. She's in pain, and—"

"Yeah, yeah. You have my blessing anyway," Tank said with a grumpy snort. "I want grandkids."

"I was massaging her back, not proposing."

"Well, speed things up a bit, then."

Chase laughed out loud. "Tank, if I date Melody, I intend to do it right."

"So . . . you're thinking about courting Melody?"

Chase glanced at the floor, then back up to meet Tank's gaze. "Okay, well, yeah, the thought has crossed my mind."

"She's a pretty little thing, all right," Tank said.

"And she's strong, intelligent, hardworking, funny . . ." Chase listed.

"Well, yeah, of course she is," Tank said. "She's my daughter, isn't she? Takes after me . . ."

"Right," Chase said crisply, stifling a chuckle. He realized Tank was in a testy mood and suspected his leg was bothering him. The older man kept reaching for the cast and tapping it with trembling fingers. Chase noticed, and his heart went out to him.

"Hey," Tank said gruffly, "did I hear you mention something about a caregiver for me? I'm not an infant, Chase, though you all seem intent on making me feel like one. Awfully presumptuous of you, making plans for me, don't you think? It's not as if you're my son-in-law yet," he said pointedly.

"Whoa, there, Tank," Chase said in measured tones. "Nobody is trying to make you feel like an infant. We're trying to get you well. Frankly, Melody is worried sick about you, and I think it's about time you took her feelings into consideration. Too, she's working herself to a frazzle, and I know you don't want her overdoing it, do you?"

Tank shot Chase a startled look. "You definitely say what's on your mind, don't you, boy?"

"Tank, you could easily fall again, and then what? You're likely to end up in the hospital, or even in a short-term care facility. Worst-case scenario, you could really mess yourself up, in which case you could end up in a long-term care facility. None of us wants that, now, do we?"

Tank watched him, wide-eyed. "I hadn't thought about that," he murmured. "I guess I could end up worse off than I already am if I'm not careful. And Melody *is* awfully tired these days. She works too hard, here and on the job," he admitted.

Chase watched Tank, curious. "Tank, do you worry about Melody, being that she's a police officer?"

"That's a stupid question," Tank said testily, but then softened. "Sorry, Chase. I'm in a foul mood, thanks to this itchy cast. Yeah, I worry, and Melody accuses me of being sexist, but it isn't that at all. If I'd had a son, I wouldn't have wanted a boy following in my footsteps either."

"Why, specifically?" Chase asked.

"Long hours, dangerous work, so much time away from the family. It's hard to find balance in our line of work, and, Lord knows, I tried."

"You don't think Melody has achieved balance?" Chase asked. She seemed like a well-rounded individual to him.

Tank chortled. "Melody's an overachiever. Always has been. She takes on everything, doesn't know when to say no, and has the kind of rush-in, ask-questions-later personality that scares the bejeebers out of me. It might be because she's still young, but then . . ."

"What?"

"She takes risks sometimes. She thinks she's invincible. She's like . . . me. The old me," he clarified.

"I hear she's darn good at her job."

"The best," Tank said proudly. "Melody doesn't do anything halfway, but, Chase, I wish I knew she was happy. I want her to be happy."

"She seems happy to me, Tank."

"But there's more to life than the job. Melody is always the first to volunteer for any assignment, doesn't balk when she takes the bulk of the call load at work, and is always willing to take a call when she should actually be winding down for the day. My fear is, she's going to burn out. And I don't want to see that happen. I really don't want to see her let life pass her by. If she wants kids, it's time she started thinking along those lines. Her biological clock is ticking."

"Tank," Chase scolded. "She has plenty of time.

She's young. Besides, people have children later in life all the time now. Heck, it's practically the norm."

"I want grandkids while I can still chase them around the lawn," Tank said, but then gave a humorless laugh. "Course, I'll need this cast off first."

The realization that Melody might want children warmed Chase. "You think Melody might want children, then?" he said tentatively.

Tank nodded. "I'm hoping anyway, and I'm also hoping she'll learn from my mistakes. Frankly, Chase, I was just like her—so gung ho about the job that I had a tendency to forget about my family when things got hectic at work. Mind you, I don't mean to suggest Melody has forgotten about me. In fact, I wish she felt she could forget about me for a while. Poor kid. I've definitely put her in a tough spot."

"She's happy to help you out," Chase told his friend. It was obvious Melody adored her father.

"I just don't want Melody to wake up someday and realize she might have missed out on the parts of life that really make a person happy."

"You mean, like a husband and children?"

Tank nodded. "I know it's Melody's decision to make—whether she decides to get married or not. If she remains single, I'll respect her choice—but I do want her to learn from my mistakes."

"What do you mean, Tank?"

"Chase, you should see my upstairs closet—full of plaques and certificates, each one commemorating my contribution to the job, and it was an honor to get them, but when all is said and done and I've left the job behind, family is what's important. It's people, Chase. People are what's important, not things, especially since things—awards, accolades—can't hug you back. It took me awhile to realize that, and I missed out on a lot during Melody's younger years."

Tank grimaced, seemingly deep in thought for a moment. "One time," he remembered, "Melody was starring in her first-grade play. She was a butterfly, and—whoa, howdy—she was excited." He smiled. "You probably don't remember this, but your mom made her costume. Anyway, I promised I'd be at that play—she made me pinky swear. You know what that is?"

Chase nodded.

"Well, you know what?"

Chase shook his head.

"I wasn't at her play, I didn't see her in her butterfly costume, and it wasn't as if something came up at work to keep me away. I just forgot. The play completely slipped my mind. I broke her heart that day, and I didn't even have a good reason. If memory serves, I was at my desk, talking on the phone to someone about something that could have easily waited until the next day. . . ."

Chase sat back in his chair and watched Tank thoughtfully. The older man swiped at his eyes and then glanced off at a point beyond Chase's head. Finally Tank broke the silence when he slapped the tabletop with the palm of his hand. "I heard you were engaged a couple of years ago, Chase."

Chase nodded slowly, surprised at Tank's swift shift in conversation.

"What happened?"

Chase smiled slightly, realizing Tank had never been a man to pull any punches either. "I wanted kids. She didn't."

Tank nodded. "You left her when she told you?"

Chase shook his head. "No, actually, I respected her decision and hoped we could make it work. Ultimately, she left me."

Tank snared his gaze. "She did you a favor. You'd have resented her for it."

"We'll never know," Chase said.

"The right girl's out there for you, Chase," Tank said with certainty. "Heck, she may very well be upstairs right now. Okay, Chase, tell me about this caregiver you have in mind for me. All my talk about family . . . well, I guess it's time I started thinking about my family—Melody."

Chapter Seven

Two weeks passed, and Melody had to admit she was pleased with the caregiver Chase had suggested. Lucy Carter, Ed's unmarried sister, had moved back to town recently, having retired from her job as a schoolteacher in a distant community. She was staying with her brother and sister-in-law until she determined what her next move would be regarding both a home of her own and part-time employment. Tank solved her unemployment problem.

Lucy had started work the day after Chase had manhandled Melody in the kitchen. Every time Melody remembered the incident, it wasn't exactly with horror. Remembering Chase's strong arms around her and his warm fingers massaging her aching back caused a warm glow to color her cheeks.

One day, Tank noticed that his daughter seemed preoccupied, and he wasn't above commenting. "Thinking about ol' Chase, aren't you?"

"What? No!"

"You could do worse, Melody."

"Pop, why are you so all-fired eager to marry me off?"

Tank tipped his head to one side, eyeing her thoughtfully. He stroked his chin. "Honey, when I'm gone—and none of us knows how much time we have on this earth—I want to know you're happily married to a good man."

"Oh, cut it out, Pop. You're not going anywhere. Spill it."

"I want grandkids while I'm young enough to enjoy them," he whined. "And I want you to be happy," he added as an afterthought.

"And you truly believe that a woman needs a man to find happiness."

"And I believe a man needs a woman to find happiness too. Everybody needs a partner."

"Well, at least you're all about reciprocity," she said sarcastically.

Melody had headed off to work then, knowing Lucy would arrive at eight and stay until one or so. While Melody still worried about her father during the afternoon and early-evening hours he spent alone, she did feel better knowing Lucy was at the house, tending to him much of the day. Since Tank was relying on the wheelchair the bulk of the time, Melody didn't worry nearly as frequently about his falling.

Lucy had proven a godsend in more ways than one. She happened to be an exceptional cook and left casseroles and other delectable dishes in the fridge for them to enjoy each evening. It was a load off Melody, not having to worry about what to prepare any longer.

Curiously, while Tank had griped constantly about Lucy the first few days she was at the house, threatening to fire the woman time and again, he'd stopped complaining and had seemingly settled into some semblance of a routine with his new caregiver.

One day, Melody had popped in to check on her father during the lunch hour and had found him and Lucy sitting together at the table, engaged in what appeared to be an intimate conversation. Her father had beamed—and had he blushed?—and Melody had wondered about it later.

But now, she had work to do. She'd already responded to multiple calls this busy Friday, bemoaning the days she griped when things were slow. Police work could be like that—excessive numbers of calls that could trickle down to nothing in a matter of mere minutes.

Then the call came over the radio to an address relatively near her house. Dispatch mentioned a burglary at the address, but, try as she might to remember, she couldn't place a house at the address specified.

Oh, well, she'd find out soon enough what was happening.

As Melody steered down a long road to an undeveloped property, she was surprised to see that someone had actually started construction on a house at the site. She furrowed her brow. Hadn't this piece of property belonged to the Carters?

Melody parked her car and stepped out carefully, since a heavy downpour earlier in the day had turned the ground into a four-wheeler's heaven. She paused, glancing ahead of her, wondering who had actually called her out. She was about to return to her car to check with dispatch when a male voice called her name.

Melody glanced up in time to see Chase striding toward her. Dressed in blue jeans, a flannel work shirt, and rain boots, he looked for all intents and purposes the rugged male, easily handsome enough to grace the cover of a sportsmen's catalogue. Melody swallowed a lump in her throat, pushing the thought aside. *Focus,* she chided herself. *Focus.*

"Hey, Melody."

"What's up, Chase? I got a call of a burglary out here."

"Yeah, come on. I'll show you," he said wearily.

Melody took a step after him and, to her chagrin, found herself ankle deep in a mud puddle. She gave a disgusted snort, lifting her boot to assess the soggy damage. The muddy water had actually topped the boot and filled the shoe. She felt a squish as she eased her foot to the ground.

"Ah, Melody, sorry about that," Chase said as he eyed the muddy mess.

"It's all right," she muttered as she attempted to sidestep a series of deep puddles in the pockmarked road. When she slipped, her knee hitting a rock, she winced in pain. Chase was at her side in a heartbeat, scooping her into his arms and carrying her to a tent-like structure within what appeared to be the start of a house foundation.

"Put me down, Chase," she moaned. "I'm on duty, for heaven's sake."

He eased her into a lawn chair beneath the tent. "I just didn't want you to fall again. Let me see your knee."

"My knee is fine," she said with a wince, rubbing her aching leg. She glanced around. "What was stolen?"

"Let's have a look at that knee first," Chase said, dropping onto his knee. He winced this time. "You tore your pants."

"Ah, great," she muttered. "It was a new uniform too."

"I don't see any blood," Chase said, as if that might make the torn uniform easier to bear. "It does look like it's going to bruise."

"I'll be fine. Tell me about this burglary."

"Can you walk?"

She nodded and rose, gingerly testing her weight on her knee. She followed Chase to a small outbuilding.

"I had tools, copper piping, some lumber, and roofing materials locked in here," he told her, "but as you can see . . ." Chased pointed at the lock that had been sliced in two.

"Looks like somebody used a bolt cutter," Melody observed. She pulled out a pocket notebook and began taking the report. Once she had the information she needed, she met his gaze with sympathetic eyes. "What was your approximate dollar loss?"

He raked a hand through his hair. "Close to two thousand. Fortunately, I hadn't brought several items out from my parent's property yet. Otherwise . . ."

"They'd be gone too. Sorry about this, Chase, but I can tell you, it happens a lot. Any time new construction pops up, we get a rash of calls from developers and builders. You'll want to be especially careful from here on out. Once they've hit you successfully, they tend to come back."

Chase sighed. "I'll keep that in mind."

"I think I have everything I need," Melody told him.

"Hey, can I show you the house, or what there is of it?" Chase said hopefully. "I've been meaning to call you, actually, but I was out of town at a week-long high school administrators' conference, and then I had to play catch-up the next week . . ."

Melody felt a slight blush tint her cheeks. She

wondered why he felt obliged to explain his absence to her. "I only have a couple of minutes, and then I'll need to get back to work."

Chase nodded and led her back to the house, which had a foundation but little else. He directed her to several features of the home, pointing out how the master bedroom was on the west side and overlooking a gorgeous mountain peak far off in the distance.

"What do you think?" he asked. "Do you think that's a good place for the master bedroom? Or would you prefer the master be on the east side, at the front of the house and overlooking the pasture?"

Melody shrugged, unsure how to respond. It was really neither here nor there to her.

"Really, Melody," he said with a hopeful smile, "I'm interested in your input."

Melody turned to look at the mountaintop, then back to the pasture. "Is there any chance the pasture may be developed soon?"

"Could be," he said. "Subdivisions seem to be popping up everywhere, even as far out as we are. I'm still surprised we've been incorporated into the city limits."

Melody furrowed her brow in thought. "I think if it were me, Chase, I'd put the master on the west side. I love a mountain view, don't you?"

He nodded, seeming satisfied, and directed her to the area of the house slated as the kitchen. "I've always liked an eat-in country kitchen," he observed. "Something with sliders or French doors opening to the backyard."

Melody nodded. She had always liked huge country kitchens too.

As Chase peppered her with questions about her preferences, she found herself interested in his descriptions of his future home, but a glance at her watch showed she had overstayed her time at the call.

"Chase, your place is going to be great, but I really need to get moving."

He nodded and walked her to her car. "Thanks for coming out," he said.

"If I learn anything about your burglars, I'll let you know."

"Do that," he said, managing a tight smile.

Melody smiled back, and Chase caught her gaze. Suddenly he leaned in and kissed her. He pressed gently, causing waves of pleasure to course through her startled system.

She was first to pull back—she was on the job, for heaven's sake. "Chase, we can't . . ."

He shook his head. "I'm sorry, Melody. I shouldn't have kissed you while you're on the job. Forgive me."

Melody watched him for a breathless moment. "Okay, then, I'll . . . get moving."

Chase nodded and watched her climb into her car, back out, and drive off. He stood as still as a statue as she disappeared around a bend. He realized he probably shouldn't have kissed Melody while she was on the job, but he couldn't seem to help himself. He hadn't planned to—it had just . . . happened.

Chase realized that he was definitely attracted to her. No two ways about it, Melody had grown into a beauty. But more than that, she was a confident, self-assured woman, and he found himself wanting to know her better.

With a faint smile still hovering on his lips, Chase strode back to the foundation that would be the groundwork for his home. One day, he would raise a family here. He had asked Melody for her input and had been pleasantly surprised that they were in agreement regarding several features of the house. That had to be good. Right?

Chapter Eight

"Pop, I'm heading to work," Melody called to her father from the kitchen several weeks later.

"Yes. Yes. Go, go," he called back, seeming to Melody to be awfully eager for her to be on her way.

She left the kitchen and found her father in his bedroom. She tapped on the door lightly before entering. "What's up, Pop?" she asked. She noted that her father was combing his hair, taking particular care with the part but growing frustrated that he couldn't seem to get it right. "Let me help you with that, Pop."

He passed her the comb, and she styled his hair quickly, passing the comb back to him. She stepped back a foot or two and noted he'd dressed carefully in dark navy pants and a coordinating striped button-down

93

shirt. He had carefully cut off the pant leg to accommodate the cast.

She wondered how he had actually managed to get dressed, since it usually involved her tugging one pant leg over his good foot, until he could reach and tug them up on his own. Melody had previously cut one pant leg off each of several pairs of his pants to accommodate the cast.

"Pop, how did you manage to get dressed on your own?"

"It wasn't easy," he admitted ruefully.

"And why did you cut the leg off a good pair of pants?" she asked. "Why aren't you wearing your sweats?"

"No reason," he said, turning away from her and wheeling himself out of the bedroom.

"Pop, you can't get away from me," she called from behind him. She caught up to him and took hold of the wheelchair. "Pop, I need to talk to you," she said in a singsong voice.

"In the kitchen," he said in a gruff voice.

In the brightly lit room, Melody saw just how nice her father looked. He'd shaved, and—Wait a minute. Did he have a haircut? She hadn't taken him for a haircut, nor had she cut his hair for him.

"Pop, who cut your hair?"

He raised a hand to his head, as if remembering his head happened to be on his neck. "Oh, uh, Lucy cut it for me. Yesterday. You didn't notice?"

"I was late getting in," she reminded him. She watched him through narrowed eyes. "Pop, do you have a lady friend? Are you carrying on with the caregiver?"

Tank's mouth dropped open. "No," he finally answered.

"Pop . . ." she persisted, watching him skeptically.

"Go to work!" He spun the chair around and headed for the living room.

"Pop, do I have to hire a chaperone now, to keep an eye on you *and* your caregiver?" she teased.

"I don't care what you do," he snapped, and Melody chuckled lightly before kissing him atop his head.

"Don't do anything I wouldn't do," she called out in warning as she headed off to work.

Unfortunately, she'd no sooner gotten on the highway than dispatch advised her of a call at the high school. She activated her emergency lights and sped to the school.

When she arrived, she found Chase in the parking lot, breaking up a fight among three boys and having a difficult time of it. While he easily held off two at a time, a third would jump into things and heat it up again. Why wasn't anyone helping him? she wondered.

Melody brought her car to a screeching halt nearby, called for backup, and then charged out of her car. She grabbed a hold of one boy so Chase could keep the other two apart. The boy fought furiously, and Melody had little choice but to spin him around, take him down on the hood of her car, and cuff him. She put him into the back of her patrol car and then jogged over to Chase.

To his surprise, Melody took hold of the bigger of the two boys who were flailing at each other furiously and yanked him away. The boy spun around to take a swing at her, but his puffy face registered shock when he noted that a police officer had a hold of him. The brief span of time gave Melody the opportunity to drop the kid, shove her knee into his back, cuff him, and then haul him back to his feet. She walked him to a separate patrol car that had just arrived. She slammed the car door closed, then registered with a wince that her back was already protesting her superhero moves.

Chase watched Melody with wide-eyed wonderment, glancing at the boy he currently had a hold of with a shocked expression on his handsome face. The look of complete surprise on his face was so comical, Melody nearly started laughing out loud. A third officer strode over to Chase then, taking the boy off his hands and into a third patrol car. He also retrieved the boy from Melody's car.

Due to the violent nature of the fight, all were eventually taken to jail, though Melody remained on the scene to take a report.

Back in Chase's office as Melody completed the incident report, Chase still watched her with unconcealed surprise.

"What?" she asked, tapping the tip of her pencil on the pad.

"I . . . I had no idea you could . . ."

"What?"

"Oh, I don't know," he murmured, raking a hand through his hair. "Uh, take down a guy twice your size?"

"Training," she said succinctly.

"Do you think you could take me?" Chase asked, seeming to come out of his stupor slightly.

"Easily," she answered, and then she rose to her feet. "I need to go. If I have additional questions, I'll call, or if you need to speak with me, call the station. See ya."

Chase watched her walk out of his office but suddenly leaped to his feet. He caught up to her and walked alongside her to her patrol car. "This is really dangerous work you do," he commented, as if he were the first to point it out to her.

She gave a brittle laugh. "I know."

"Why do you do it?" he ventured. "Melody, something could go wrong, and it could be over for you. Look at what happened to Tank."

"The situation with Pop could have happened off the job just as easily, and, frankly, your job has the potential to be dangerous too. Did you forget I just found you attempting to break up a fight among three very belligerent teens?"

"But I'm a man. . . ."

Melody stopped in her tracks and spun around. *"Did you just say . . . ?"*

He raised a hand as if in surrender. "Did I just say that? Wow! Melody, I didn't mean anything by that. Really, I didn't. I know a woman is as capable as a man in any field. If I thought differently, I don't belong in a school setting. But I'm just wondering if you've ever considered a different line of work."

She wondered how much to divulge to him. She hadn't made any concrete decisions relating to her work, but she had been doing a lot of thinking. "Truthfully, I've been thinking about getting off the streets and doing something different for the department, but I'm not sure yet. I'll always do something in law enforcement, however," she told him. "How about you, Chase?" she asked him pointedly.

"Would I consider a different line of work?" he mused aloud. "Probably not. I'd probably always do something in education. I like kids. Do you?"

"What?" she asked distractedly. "Oh, like kids, you mean? Uh, sure. They're darling when they're little, but as you well know, they grow up." She gave a shudder, and Chase eyed her curiously.

"What if you had a family, Melody? What if you had children of your own? Would you still remain in law enforcement?"

She hadn't given much thought to whether or not she would give up the job to have a family. It wasn't as if the opportunity had presented itself—truthfully, she was too busy for the opportunity to have ever presented itself.

If she had children, she knew she wouldn't be nearly so eager to put her life on the line day in and day out. Of course, if she ever did have children, she could still remain in law enforcement. She could go into probation or another line of work not quite so dangerous. But she had to acknowledge, law enforcement was inherently dangerous. It just was.

"I have to go, Chase," Melody said, eager to escape Chase's probing eyes. Sometimes he had a way of looking at her that made her think he could see right through her.

She slipped into the driver's seat, but Chase took hold of the door. "Melody, will you have dinner with me tonight?"

"What?"

"Will you have dinner with me tonight?"

She glanced up and met his gaze just as a lanky teen happened to walk over to them, raising his hand to Chase for a high five. Chase slapped the boy's hand but then furrowed his brow.

"Ethan, aren't you supposed to be in class?"

The boy grinned sheepishly. "On my way."

"Glad to hear it," Chase said, watching the boy to assure himself that Ethan entered the building and didn't detour to the nearby football stadium. He knew that several students often took off for the stadium when they were supposed to be in class. Satisfied that Ethan was where he should be, Chase turned back to Melody.

"Will you have dinner with me tonight?"

Melody grinned and opened her mouth to speak but suddenly caught sight of two kids striding across the field to the stadium.

"Chase, look." She nodded toward the students, who were now jogging toward the off-limits stadium.

"Ah, shoot," Chase muttered. "I need to deal with them right now."

"I know. I'll talk to you later."

It wasn't until she was out of sight that Chase realized she hadn't given him an answer about dinner.

Chase left work early so he could spend some time at his property, then headed home at about five-thirty to clean up. He had attempted to contact Melody at the station an hour ago, to get that answer about dinner out together, but he had been told she was busy. He'd left a message but as yet hadn't heard back from her.

After taking a quick shower at home and dressing in a pair of nice jeans and a red polo shirt, he drove to Melody's to see if she was up for dinner. When he arrived, he found Tank and his aunt on the front porch, sipping a drink he couldn't readily identify and so engrossed in conversation that they didn't even notice him as he practically tumbled onto the porch.

"Watch that last step," he said to no one in particular.

"Chase," Tank said, extending a hand to him and seeming relatively pleased to see him.

His aunt, on the other hand, didn't look quite so pleased, even when he kissed her on the cheek. "Hey,

Aunt Lucy," he greeted her. He dropped into a chair beside her, leaning forward and resting his elbows on his knees. "Anything new and exciting going on?" he asked.

He didn't miss the slightly horrified expression that crossed his aunt's face, nor did he miss how gussied up Tank appeared to be, nor did he miss the fact that his aunt had apparently stayed with Tank well beyond her customary work hours. Wow, he thought to himself, he didn't miss much.

"Awfully nice weather we're having," he commented, and his aunt nodded a bit too curtly.

"Nice," Tank repeated, and Chase leaned toward him, as if pulled by an invisible string.

"Tank, buddy, you have something on your mouth. . . ." Chase pointed at the blotch of color staining the big man's lips. "What is that?" He narrowed his eyes, trying to see, and then his eyes widened. A quick glance at his aunt's lips confirmed his suspicions. Yep, same color as the blotch on Tank's mouth. Whoa.

Chase couldn't manage to erase the goofy grin that had spread across his face. "I, uh, suppose I really should get moving," he said, and the couple seemed downright relieved.

"Did you need something?" Tank asked then, almost as an afterthought.

"I stopped by to see if Melody would have dinner with me, but . . ."

Tank glanced at Lucy, and if Chase hadn't been

watching his aunt so intently, he might have missed her almost imperceptible nod.

"Tonight? You want to take her out tonight?" Tank asked hopefully.

"Yes, tonight."

Suddenly Tank seemed downright giddy, and his aunt appeared to fight the soft smile that quirked her not-as-pink-as-they-had-been lips. "Melody should be home by six, give or take—well, unless she takes on an overtime shift. If not, I'm sure she'd love to go out to dinner with you," Tank said enthusiastically.

"Oh, I don't know about that," Chase admitted, tipping back his chair.

"Why would you say that?" Lucy said, becoming the protective aunt in a flash. "You're a wonderful boy."

"I'm a wonderful man," Chase corrected with a grin. "But I asked her out earlier and couldn't get an answer from her." Suddenly his eyes widened, and he turned to Tank. "Tank, is Melody dating someone? I'd hate to . . ."

Tank shook his head. "Nope, she's all yours. No worries about stepping on anybody's toes."

Chase chuckled at that. He doubted Melody would appreciate her father's suggesting she belonged to anyone.

"So, Chase, did you plan on waiting here for Melody to arrive, or were you going to go somewhere and kill some time?" his aunt asked sweetly.

Fortunately, to Chase's relief and to the that of couple sitting with him on the porch, Melody pulled up then, her tires crunching the gravel in the driveway. She glanced up curiously, noting Lucy was still there.

As she climbed out of the car and approached the porch, she smiled at Lucy. "How are you, Lucy?" she inquired.

"Very well, dear," the woman said.

Melody turned to Chase and then her father. "Chase? Pop?"

"I'm fine," Chase said.

"Good. Real good," Tank said.

Melody nodded, then leaned closer to her father. "Pop, you have something pink on your mouth." She leaned forward for a closer look, and her eyes widened. She turned to Lucy and spied the very same shade on the woman's lips.

Chase was still tipped back in the chair but was nodding his head up and down in confirmation of Melody's discovery. "I need a word with you Melody," Chase said then, bringing his chair legs forward with a smack. "In the kitchen. Okay?"

Numbly, Melody followed him into the house.

"I know, I know," Chase said, watching her with a sympathetic expression when they reached the kitchen. "I was shocked too. Tank and Aunt Lucy have really only known each other for a few weeks, and they're already locking lips. But, since your father is a broken man, literally, I say we let him have his fun."

Melody opened her mouth to speak but promptly clamped it shut.

Chase sat down at the dinette table and waited for Melody to find her voice. It wasn't long.

"They . . . they haven't known each other long enough to be kissing!" Melody shook her head in exasperation. "They were kissing, Chase!"

"I know!"

"I'm not sure what I think about this," Melody admitted as she dropped into a chair.

"Can we talk about it over dinner?" Chase suggested with a sympathetic smile.

"We're not going to dinner. Lord knows, those two need chaperones, and I, for one, do not plan on leaving them alone—ever!"

Chase reached across the table and took Melody's hand. "Melody, I think we should let them be. How much trouble can Tank get into with his bum leg? I'm sure Aunt Lucy can outrun 'im."

"Chase!" Melody said, aghast.

"Listen, Mel, they want an evening alone. Frankly, they want the two of us to hit the road. I say we let them have their evening together. Come on. Tank seems . . . happy. And I'm glad to see it."

Melody swallowed a lump in her throat. Her father wanted her gone so he could have time alone with a woman? How did she feel about her father dating? She just wasn't sure. Her beloved mother had been gone only three short years. . . .

"Why don't you run upstairs and change?" Chase said, interrupting her thoughts. "They're really chomping at the bit to get us gone. We can talk at the restaurant."

"Okay," Melody said numbly as she walked like a robot to her room and dropped her duty belt onto her bed. She eased the .45 caliber out of the holster and locked it in the small gun safe. Next, she slipped out of her clothes and down to her underwear and then checked her closet for an outfit, but she realized she hadn't a clue where Chase planned on taking her.

She walked to the door, cracking it open a bit. "Chase," she called loudly, "where are we going?"

"Anywhere you want to go," he called back.

In that case, she put on jeans, a soft pink sweater, and slip-on shoes. She refreshed her makeup, combed her hair, and padded out of her room. Chase waited for her in the kitchen.

"Are you sure we should leave them, Chase?" Melody asked with concern. "I feel like I should give them the birds-and-the-bees talk first."

Chase laughed. "They'll be fine."

Chapter Nine

Melody sat across from Chase in the booth, seeming to stare straight through him as she bit into her burger.

"You know," Chase said, "I would have sprung for something a little more upscale than the Burger Barn. I do enjoy fine dining on occasion."

She waved off his concern. "I love this place." She picked up her large paper cup and attempted to sip a strawberry milkshake through the straw.

"But how am I going to woo you in a place like this?" he asked.

Melody glanced up. "Huh?"

Chase laughed with chagrin. "Melody, this is our first real date, and you're light-years away. It's not doing much for my fragile ego."

Melody grimaced, felt bad for a fleeting second, and then realized Chase's ego was faring just fine, as evidenced by the lingering glances he was receiving from nearly every woman in the place.

"Your ego is fine," she snapped. "And stop grinning at all those women."

"I'm not grinning *at* them, but I am smiling *back* at them, in acknowledgment of their acknowledgment of me. I can't be rude," he said. "I'm the new high school principal, and they can't help but be curious about me. Besides, I'm told I'm the most eligible bachelor in town."

"What?" Melody said, a smile pulling at her lips. "Who told you that?"

"I take it you disagree, then?"

Melody laughed outright. "I didn't say I disagreed. . . ."

"Good!" Chase said with relief. "I've finally managed to get a smile out of you."

"That was more a guffaw than a smile," Melody pointed out. "So, you're the most eligible bachelor in town, are you?"

"According to my mother . . ." he said in measured tones.

Melody really laughed then, but as a result she felt a stabbing pain in her middle back. She shifted slightly in the hard booth.

"Are you okay?" Chase asked, watching her with concern. "Is your back bothering you? Do you need me to massage it?"

"No, I don't need you to massage my back," she said testily, and she realized she'd snapped at him. "I'm sorry, Chase," she murmured. "I know I'm in a bad mood. I'm just not sure how I feel about Pop's dating."

"Aunt Lucy's a fine woman," he pointed out. "I'm told she has a tidy nest egg too. Tank could do worse."

Melody shot Chase an alarmed glance, then chuckled. "Are you suggesting my father is a gold digger?"

"Of course not." Chase laughed.

"I know Lucy's a wonderful person," Melody said. She didn't want Chase thinking she didn't like his aunt. In fact, she liked her just fine, but . . . She was lost to her thoughts, and Chase watched the emotions crisscross her face. "I know he's going to date eventually. . . ." she murmured.

Chase nodded. "Tank isn't even sixty yet, is he?"

Melody shook her head.

"He's got a lot of life left in him. You know, the truth is, I think Aunt Lucy has been good for him. My mom mentioned to me that Tank hadn't been himself lately, even aside from the injured leg."

"Hmm," Melody said, but she knew that Chase was right. Her father hadn't been himself since her mother passed away. But lately he seemed . . . happier.

Melody finished her burger and pushed the empty plastic wicker basket away from her. She hadn't ordered fries, but suddenly she felt hungry for them. She reached across the table and took several from Chase's basket.

Finally she looked up, glancing around her. The burger joint was full, with people standing as they waited for tables to open up. "Shall we get out of here?" she suggested.

Chase nodded, and they rose from the table. He draped an arm around Melody's shoulders as they left the restaurant. Chase checked his watch. "It's early yet. Would you like to take a walk?"

Melody nodded, and together they strolled along the street. Neither spoke for several moments.

"Let's go to the park," Chase suggested, indicating the park just ahead.

He took her hand, and they stepped onto the mat of perfectly shorn grass in the city park. It was like a carpet, and Melody knew that the city planners prided themselves on the beauty of this particular park.

The couple sat beneath a tree, enjoying the cool evening breeze.

"Are you okay, Melody?" Chase asked finally. "Are you warm enough?"

He noted she hugged her arms around her body, and he wished he'd thought to bring a light jacket.

"I'm fine," she assured him. "Hey, I'm sorry I'm such bad company tonight. I don't know why Pop's dating has thrown me for such a loop. I mean, I'm . . . okay with it," she said, sounding as if she hoped to convince herself as much as him.

"Well, good. I'm glad. The fact is, if Tank and Lucy have chemistry, then we should be happy for them."

"Chemistry . . . ?" Melody murmured.

Chase reached a gentle finger to Melody's chin and tipped her face toward him. "Do you think you and I might have some chemistry?" he asked, his eyes alight with humor.

Melody was taken aback and didn't immediately answer him.

"Really, Melody," he prompted. "Do you feel anything for me?"

"I . . . I don't know," she admitted. "I mean, it's good to see you . . . and . . ."

Chase chuckled. "It's good to see you too. Oh, man, my ego is taking a beating tonight." He leaned back in the grass, propping himself up on one elbow. He watched Melody with a slightly bemused expression on his face. "Well, you used to like me anyway."

"What do you mean, Chase?" Melody asked. "I . . . I still like you."

Chase eyed her speculatively. "Well, it's something to build on," he said somewhat mysteriously, and then he pulled Melody toward him. He kissed her gently on the lips, pressing with an exquisite insistency, and suddenly Melody forgot all about Tank and Lucy. And although she didn't think about chemistry, she realized later that she and Chase had plenty of it.

Chase took her home by ten-thirty, since they both had early mornings the next day. As Chase steered his truck into the drive in front of her house and parked, Melody turned to him, watching him but seeming to stare right through him.

"Something on your mind?" he asked. "You seem preoccupied."

"No. I'm fine. Thanks for tonight. I had fun."

She had, she realized, had fun with Chase. She wouldn't have believed she would have been in any frame of mind to have fun, but the evening had surprised her. He had surprised her.

Chase clasped her hand in his, giving it a gentle squeeze. "I had fun too."

Melody was quiet, seemingly lost to her thoughts again.

"What are you thinking now?" Chase asked.

"I was thinking about my mother," she told him, smiling as if at a fond memory.

"I know you miss her. My mom talks about her all the time."

"They were best friends," Melody uttered.

She glanced at Chase, remembering the past. She and Chase had been friends as children, though the five-year age difference had been huge once Chase hit his teens. Prior to that, he had treated Melody like the little sister he had always wanted, and she had regarded him as a brother, until . . .

Melody cringed, recalling the onset of hormones. It hadn't helped that Chase was tall, dark, and handsome even as a young teen. In fact, as the star quarterback on his football team, center on his basketball team, and pitcher on his baseball team, he had been the town's equivalent to a movie star as far as Melody was concerned.

When Chase had been crowned king at nearly every dance during his four years in high school, it had only added to his masculine mystique. He was a brightly shining star in the town and in Melody's life. When he went off to college, she had been devastated—as if the light had been turned off.

Melody sighed, and Chase reached for her, pulling her close to him. She didn't protest, surprised to realize she was glad for his arms around her. He didn't try to kiss her lips but instead gave her a chaste kiss on the top of her head. He held her close for several moments until, finally, she pulled away.

She turned to face him. "I'm being silly, huh?"

"I don't think so," he told her.

Chase brushed a kiss across her cheek and then climbed out of the cab. He rounded the truck and opened her door, extending a hand to help her down. Once her feet touched the ground, he caught her gaze, searching her face, and then he leaned down and brushed his lips against hers. When he wrapped her in an embrace, she leaned against him, finding solace in his strong arms.

"Thanks for dinner," she told him when she pulled back.

"Can we do it again sometime soon?" he asked, and then he chuckled. "And may I pick the restaurant?"

Melody smiled. "Sure, we can go out again. And, yes, you can pick the restaurant." She turned then and let herself into the house. She closed the door behind her and then paused for a moment. She had had a good time with Chase, despite her concerns about her father. She still felt the warmth of Chase's lips against her own.

Oh, my, she thought suddenly, was she falling for Chase Carter again? Was history repeating itself, as it so often did?

"How was your date, Pop?" Melody asked her father the next morning over a breakfast of bacon, eggs, and toast.

He glanced up, his expression startled.

"Come on, Pop, it was pretty obvious you and Lucy wanted some time alone together."

"Well, the truth is, it was really good." He watched her speculatively then. "Hon, you and I haven't really discussed the subject of my dating, have we?"

"No, we haven't," she admitted, reaching for a slice of toast.

"How . . . do you feel about it?" he asked, seeming to hold his breath in anticipation of her response.

"Pop, I admit, it's hard for me, but . . . You have every right to find happiness with someone. You're still a young guy."

"Well, not too young," he said with a short laugh, "but I appreciate that, Melody. What about you? Any chance you and Chase might be hitting it off?" Tank asked hopefully.

She laughed. "Um, well, yeah."

She smiled dreamily, and Tank noticed. A wide grin spread across his face.

"Okay, Pop," Melody warned when she saw his hopeful expression, "don't get any ideas. It's too early for you to even be thinking what I suspect you're thinking."

"But you like him?"

"Yeah, I do. He wants to take me to dinner again soon."

"Are you going?" her father asked eagerly.

"Well, I told him yes—that we could go out again."

"In that case, could you go tonight?" her father asked, watching her with imploring eyes.

Melody shook her head. "Are you serious, Pop?"

"Well, yeah. Lucy and I want to rent a scary movie tonight. We plan to order a pizza, eat popcorn, and drink sodas. It should be a good time."

"Sounds like it," Melody said softly.

"Would you mind stopping by the pizza place and bringing home the largest all-meat combination they have on the menu?" her father asked.

Melody chuckled ruefully. "Anything you want, Pop."

"Maybe you should call Chase about dinner out tonight," Tank suggested eagerly.

"Pop, I can manage to be out of the house without Chase's factoring into the equation."

"Hey, is that math talk? And unless I didn't make myself clear last night, I'd love to go out with you again, Melody."

The deep voice from the doorway prompted Melody to spin around in her chair.

"The door was open," Chase answered in response to her raised eyebrows.

"How ya doin', Chase?" Tank inquired cheerfully.

Chase immediately sensed that Tank was in good spirits. "Did my aunt put that smile on your face, Tank?" he asked. "Cause if so, I might have to sock you in the mouth. Hard."

"We simply enjoy each other's company," Tank assured him. "Besides, in my current physical state, I couldn't catch up with her to do anything that would put a smile on my face."

"We saw the lipstick on your mouth, remember," Chase and Melody said unison.

Tank chuckled. "Well, aside from a little smooching . . ."

"I have to go," Melody said, her eyes widening. "I really have to go."

She pushed back from the table and met Chase's steady gaze. "You wanna go to dinner tonight?" she asked with a smile. "I'm buying."

"Yep, but I should warn you, my tastes are more expensive than yours."

"I'll consider myself warned."

"Six all right with you both?" Tank asked sweetly.

Chase picked Melody up a few minutes before six, and to her surprise, they drove to a seafood restaurant in a town a half hour away. As they settled into their seats, Melody checked out their surroundings. A nautical theme abounded, with fishnets strewn about, capturing colorful plastic fish and shiny rubber lobsters. A massive anchor spanned a nearby wall. Even their seats were fashioned from cushions placed comfortably within tiny fishing boats.

"Fine dining, eh?' Melody said with a chuckle.

"You don't like seafood?" Chase inquired. "I happen to know that this place has excellent snow crab."

Melody nodded distractedly, glancing again at their surroundings. She turned back and found Chase watching her intently. "What?" she said.

"I was just thinking how beautiful you are," he replied.

"Right," she said with a laugh. "Really, what's on your mind?"

"I just told you."

Melody was glad when the waitress appeared, passing them menus and then taking their beverage orders. Melody ordered a cherry Coke, and Chase followed suit.

Melody studied the menu, finally snapping it closed. "What are you having?" Chase asked.

"Snow crab."

"Me too."

The twosome sat quietly, and Melody noted that Chase suddenly seemed preoccupied. She commented, and he smiled sadly. "I was just remembering a meeting I had today. I received word that the school district is considering canceling a dance at the high school in a couple of weeks because, apparently, there's been a good deal more than dancing going on at the past few dances."

"Such as?" Melody inquired with interest, although she could certainly imagine. She herself had often responded to calls at the high school during evening events there, prior to returning to a day-shift position at work.

"Drinking, fighting, smoking . . . all manner of activities that don't belong at a high school dance," Chase listed in answer to her question. "It's a shame. These kids grow up too fast, and, frankly, I think these dances and other extracurricular activities are important for them. They can create memories that last a lifetime."

Melody watched Chase, a slight smile lifting the corners of her lips. She hadn't given the matter much thought. Although she had gone to an occasional dance during high school, at the time she had been more interested in riding the horse she owned or spending time at her father's job, accompanying various officers on ride-alongs. She realized with chagrin that her father probably would have preferred that she spend her time at a dance, rather than in the front seat of a patrol car, responding to dangerous calls alongside full-time officers.

"I hope I was able to persuade the powers-that-be how important the dances are to many of these kids," Chase commented.

His words brought Melody back to the present. "What did you say to persuade them?"

"Actually, I suggested we have local law enforcement present, in addition to the one security officer who typically patrols the parking lot. I think having police officers there will go a long way toward keeping problems at bay."

"Maybe," Melody mused. "Have you spoken to anyone at the department about it?"

He nodded. "I talked to James Moore today. He's a friend from high school."

Melody grinned widely. "James is my sergeant."

"Really? Small world. Small town," he added ruefully. "James graduated a couple of years ahead of me, but we played football and baseball together."

Melody nodded. "What did James say about your idea?"

"He said he'll take it up with his commander and get back to me."

Chapter Ten

A week had passed since her date with Chase. Melody arrived back at the station after another hectic day of calls. Before she signed out for the day, she needed to complete a complex incident report relating to an identity-theft ring in town. She began the tedious process of formulating the report, attempting to keep names straight. Since the subjects each had so many aliases, it was nearly impossible. She growled in frustration, and her sergeant glanced over at her as he stepped into the room.

"How's it going, Mel?" he inquired.

"Not so good," she grumbled. "These identity-theft reports aren't fun."

"Don't I know it," he agreed. "Hey, don't forget to

check out the mandatory overtime sheets. I made some changes."

She nodded absently, her attention now focused completely on her report. Finally, with a second proofreading of her efforts and a big sigh of relief, she filed the report and stood from the desk. She stretched her back, which still felt tight.

Remembering that Sarge had mentioned the mandatory OT sheet, she ambled over for a look before she headed home. Although the OT *was* mandatory, officers were given a choice as to what assignment they wanted to work on a first-come, first-served basis. Those who didn't act quickly were stuck with whatever happened to be left over.

Melody noticed that a new list had been added and that apparently Chase had gotten his wish that local officers be on hand at school events. She noted that a dance the following weekend would be manned by two officers. Her eyes widened when she realized she was one of the two.

Wait a minute! She'd signed up for overtime at the motocross event the same night. The popular event was always a rousing good time, with fights erupting between participants and spectators alike. Melody got a charge out of the event, though her father bemoaned her going.

Melody dashed into her sergeant's office, catching him just as he was shrugging into a light jacket and heading out the door.

"Uh, Sarge, you have a minute?"

"Sure, Mel, what's up?"

"I just saw the OT list, and I've been moved from the motocross event to the high school dance."

He nodded. "Yeah, we had to make some changes."

"But . . . I was at the top of the list for the motocross, so why was I moved?" Before he could answer, she posed another question. "Did Chase Carter have something to do with this?"

Her sergeant looked aghast, or at least pretended to. "Well, no, actually. Commander Manchester thought you and Benton were the logical choices for a school event, since you're both young and . . ." He grinned, choosing his words carefully. "Because you're young and more likely to relate well to the students than some of us old fogies would."

"I'd really like to go to the motocross."

He grinned knowingly. "I know you look forward to the motocross event—don't we all?" he added with a grin. "But sometimes ya gotta do what ya gotta do, Mel."

Melody nodded, tight-lipped and unhappy at the turn of events. She hadn't particularly enjoyed school dances when she was a kid. The prospect of spending an evening at one at the ripe old age of twenty-eight certainly didn't appeal to her. Frankly, the assignment equated to babysitting, and she was light-years beyond babysitting too.

She couldn't help but wonder again, did Chase have something to do with the change in her OT assignment?

Melody headed home, not particularly surprised to find Lucy still there.

"Are you hungry, Melody?" Lucy asked. "I made lasagna—old family recipe."

Melody paused for a brief moment in the doorway to the kitchen. "Thanks, Lucy, but I think I'll pass. You two enjoy yourselves."

Her father watched her curiously, but she averted her gaze and headed up to her room. She didn't especially want to spend her evening holed up in her room, but she just didn't feel like joining her father and his lady friend for dinner. It occurred to her that she might want to consider making the move back out to the small house on the property, but she knew it wouldn't be prudent, considering she needed to be within earshot of her father during nighttime hours.

She remembered a night a couple of weeks after her father had had his first surgery. He'd had a hard plaster cast at that point, and his leg had somehow dropped off the bed, and, unfortunately, the rest of him had followed it to the floor. He had landed with a horrendous thud, and had she not been staying in the house, things could have turned out very badly.

Melody shed her work clothes and dressed in shorts and a tank top. She made a quick decision to go for a jog to clear her head and then considered whether or not to drive into town after. She knew she could use a few toiletry items from the drugstore.

Melody headed downstairs and out the front door,

calling out a good-bye to Tank and Lucy. She jogged down the lane to the main roadway, crossed carefully, and then continued, enjoying the sensation of freedom. A light wind whipped her hair back and felt cool and invigorating against her skin. She kept up a rigorous pace, though not as quick as she normally ran. Her knee throbbed occasionally, her back still felt as if the muscles were clenched up, and she was disgruntled to realize that one shoulder protested periodically as she pumped her arms. She was a mess, she realized.

Nonetheless, she jogged onward, her thin, shapely legs eliciting a honk or two from passersby. She chuckled each time. It was good for the ego, but when a truck passed, suddenly hit the brakes, and pulled to the side of the road and parked, she became slightly alarmed. She brought herself to an abrupt halt and watched the vehicle through narrowed eyes.

With hands on her hips, she endeavored to control her breathing, wondering what action she might be forced to take. She reached for the pepper spray in her pocket, keeping both her hand and the spray hidden within the pocket, one finger poised and ready to deploy the fiery formula. With her other hand she reached for her cell phone. She grimaced. She'd left it charging on her bedside table.

By now, dusk was beginning to settle, and she couldn't make out the driver of the vehicle, who remained behind the wheel. She could tell it was a man, but he didn't seem particularly eager to exit the vehicle.

She couldn't help but wonder what was up. She chose not to hang around and find out. First, she committed the plate to memory—just in case—and then she turned, crossed the highway, and ran in the opposite direction.

To her surprise, the truck suddenly did a U-turn, pulling just ahead of her and stopping. She saw an arm jut out the driver's side window and wave her over. Wow, this guy was persistent, she thought. She pulled the pepper spray out this time, fully ready to use it.

She walked carefully toward the truck, veering right of it to pass, and then cast a sidelong glance at the driver.

Chase!

He sat behind the wheel, his cell phone pressed to his ear. He motioned her over. She shook her head, grimacing with both anger and frustration. The man was fortunate she didn't jog over and douse him with the spray for putting her through such a frightening ordeal. She waved a hand dismissively and then continued on her jog—though she headed for home this time. Chase had definitely taken the fun out of her run.

She wasn't especially surprised when he soon pulled in front of her again, this time exiting the vehicle and meeting her beside his truck. "Why didn't you stop?" he demanded.

"Why *did* you stop?" she retorted angrily. "Chase Carter, you scared the daylights out of me back there. Why'd you stay in the truck? I didn't know it was you."

"I'm sorry," he said sincerely. "I got an important call from school and had to take it. But I figured you'd recognize my truck."

"Well, I didn't," she said crossly. "It's getting dark."

"I'm really sorry," he said.

She shot him an exasperated glance. "Yeah, okay, well, I have to go." She turned to leave, but he gently took her arm and watched her with concerned eyes.

"Do you always jog this late in the evening, Melody?"

"Sometimes, why?"

"It's, uh, not particularly safe—a young woman out here alone."

"I'm not so young, and, frankly, I'm growing older by the second." How dare he question her ability to take care of herself? She'd had hours of training in one-on-one combat, and she could take down just about anybody. He knew that. With a withering glance at him, she started off again.

To her surprise, he jogged beside her for several yards before she pulled to a stop and stared at him. "What are you doing?"

"Jogging with you."

She surveyed his clothing, taking in the navy slacks, white button-down shirt, and tie. And the shoes! Probably Italian leather and likely with slippery soles.

"Chase, get back to your truck."

"I'm not leaving you alone out here. It's getting dark."

She glared at him, then pressed her eyelids shut. She forced herself to take a deep, calming breath. "Chase," she said reasonably, "I jog alone all the time. I've never had a problem until . . . you!"

"Well, Melody, as my mother always says, there's a first time for everything. Really, Melody, it's getting dark, and you don't have any reflective tape on. You could be hit by a car, or some weirdo could easily grab you."

Melody stood as still as a statue, but suddenly her eyes widened as an idea formed in her frustrated brain. In the blink of an eye, she grasped Chase by the hand, spun him around, raked a foot across his ankle, and pushed with superhuman strength—fueled by frustration. Once she had him on the ground, she dropped onto his back, forcing her knee between his shoulder blades. To cap off her surprise attack, she twisted his hand, eliciting a pained groan from him.

"Chase," she said sweetly, "I just demonstrated to you what would happen to anyone who tried to mess with me," she said with a satisfied snort.

"What if the someone had a gun or a knife?" Chase asked. "What would you do then?" His voice sounded muffled, but it would, she realized, with his face pressed against the concrete roadway.

"I guess I'd cross that bridge when I came to it," Melody told him honestly.

Melody heard his muffled but skeptical chuckle,

which prompted her to twist his hand a bit for painful emphasis. She leaned close to his ear. "Say uncle."

"Nope."

"I'm not letting you up until you say uncle."

"We could be here all night," he replied, still chuckling. "I have some pride, you know."

"Still think I can't handle myself, Chase Carter?"

"I never said you couldn't handle yourself, Melody Hudson."

Melody released his hand and stood up abruptly, having effectively made her point. She could take Chase, or any other man, who tried to mess with her.

Chase rose from the concrete, brushing off his pants and glancing at her with barely concealed amusement. If he didn't get that smug grin off his face, she might wipe it off for him.

"What are you so smug about?" she demanded hotly. "I just took you down, and, frankly, it was oh, so easy."

"Uh-huh." Chase continued to dust off his clothing, then rubbed at a scuff on his shoe. He finally glanced up and snared her gaze. To her utter and complete surprise, he lunged, scooping her off the ground and tossing her over his shoulder like a sack of potatoes. She struggled initially but stopped. She knew she could escape his hold, but doing so might result in his disfigurement. And she really didn't want to harm his face. As annoying as the man was at present, he was arguably the best-looking man she'd seen in a long while.

Chase strode to the truck and deposited Melody on the front seat. She sat, facing out the open passenger door, and Chase planted himself in front of her, watching her with that same smug expression she'd seen a moment before. "What do you have to say for yourself now, Melody?" he asked, watching her with a triumphant gleam in his eyes. "You weren't able to get away from me just then."

She sighed as if bored and studied her fingernails. "I didn't try."

He seemed taken aback. "Wouldn't have mattered if you did."

She shook her head, as if to convey just how delusional he was. "Chase, had I tried to get away, I easily could have done so. However . . ." She paused for emphasis. "I felt it best to leave your face intact—as well as other parts of your body I suspect you prize as much."

He snickered, but then his eyebrows furrowed into a frown. "Oh," he said softly, appearing thoughtful. Suddenly he perked up. "So . . . you like my face?"

"I didn't say that," she said with a neither-here-nor-there shrug. "But I do love your parents, and, curiously, they do seem rather fond of you, so I'd hate to be responsible for rearranging your face."

Chase cocked his head to one side. "Okaaaay, then," he said, but he remained in front of her, watching her with an expression she couldn't quite read.

"What?" she demanded.

He laughed and raked a hand through his hair. "I just think . . ."

"What?" she demanded again.

"You're an amazing woman, Melody Hudson."

"Oh!" she said, unable to fight the grin that spread across her face. To her surprise, Chase leaned in and kissed her, and she found herself responding as he deepened the kiss.

When an eighteen-wheeler roared past and laid on the horn, they both nearly jumped out of their skin.

"We'd better go," Chase said, pulling back and smiling into her eyes.

"Yes, we should."

With a gentle hand, Chase urged her to swing her legs into the truck so he could close the door. He rounded the front of the truck and climbed into the driver's seat. Before starting it up, he turned to her with sincere eyes. "Melody, I am sorry I scared you. I didn't mean to."

"Apology accepted," she told him.

"Where to?" Chase asked.

Melody supposed she should head home, though she wasn't especially eager. "Home, I guess."

Chase shot her a speculative glance as he started the truck. "We could head by my folks' place so I can change, and then, if you're up to it, we could go grab a bite at the Burger Barn."

She considered the offer. "Why not?" she said with a shrug. "I'm always up for a juicy burger."

They rode in silence for a couple of minutes, and Chase noticed Melody frowning. "Something wrong?" he asked.

She shook her head. "Nothing really."

"Bad day at work?"

"Not really. Just long." Suddenly she remembered having been removed from the motocross assignment and reassigned to work the high school dance. "Hey, Chase," she began, eyeing him speculatively, "you didn't ask Sergeant Moore to assign me to work the school dance, did you?"

He shook his head. "No. Why?"

"No reason," she murmured, and she turned her head to stare out the windshield. Neither she nor Chase spoke as he steered his truck to his parents' farm.

He parked, and they climbed out of the truck, Melody refusing to wait for Chase to round the vehicle and open her door. They walked together up the porch steps and into his parents' living room.

"Mom! Dad!" Chase called.

When no one answered, he turned to Melody. "Seems we have the place to ourselves. I'm going to get out of these clothes, and then I'll be right back. Make yourself comfortable."

Melody dropped onto the floral print sofa, glancing around the room. She knew virtually every nook and cranny of the place, having spent countless hours visiting the Carters along with her parents.

She rose from the couch; moving to check out the

photos on the fireplace mantel. Photos of Chase lined the space, from his babyhood until adulthood. He'd been an adorable baby who had grown into an incredibly handsome man.

Melody reached for a photo of Chase at eighteen. She studied it, taking in the dark, curly hair, twinkling brown eyes, and wide smile. She realized this was how she had remembered him—at least until the real thing showed up in town weeks before.

She returned the photo to the mantel when Chase stepped into the room. "Cute, wasn't I?" he commented.

Melody couldn't help but chuckle. "Adorable. What happened?"

Chase leveled his gaze at her. "You think I'm handsome. I see it in your baby blues every time you glance my way."

"You are so arrogant!" she cried, harrumphing in disgust.

"I can be," he admitted good-naturedly. "So can you. Hey, I'm thinking, you seem tired, and I'm feeling a little weary myself. Wanna check out the fridge and see what Mom left for me?"

"I can head home and grab something," she offered. "I'm sure you have things to do."

"No, join me. I'll be lonely if you go."

Melody followed him into the kitchen. Chase pulled open the fridge and found a meatloaf and mashed potatoes. There was also a bowl full of cold biscuits.

He pulled the items from the fridge and then retrieved

plates from the cupboard. He spooned out the food, putting a plate into the microwave, and then the next one after the first had heated up. He passed a plate to Melody before quickly warming the biscuits. After retrieving butter and jam from the fridge, he joined Melody at the table.

"Looks good," she said, and it did. Chase's mom could cook like nobody's business.

The twosome ate in silence. Finally, Chase spoke. "What's on your mind, Melody? You're awfully quiet."

"Have you noticed you always ask me what I'm thinking?" she pointed out. "What are *you* thinking about?"

"My shoes. My . . . brand . . . new . . . shoes."

Melody winced. "New? Feel free to send me a bill."

"Naw, I had it coming. I should have figured you'd kick me to the curb, literally. And you didn't disappoint."

"I am sorry about the shoes."

"Not a problem. You want to go for a walk?" he asked her when they finished their dinner and deposited the dirty dishes into the sink.

"Not really," she admitted. "I should go home."

"It's early," he pointed out. "Besides, my folks are at your place."

"And how do you know that?"

He pointed at a note tacked to the fridge. " 'Having dinner with Tank and Lucy. Food in the fridge. Love, Mom.' I just noticed it."

"Oh."

Melody pushed back from the table. She walked into the living room, glancing around. To her surprise, Chase came up behind her and wrapped his arms around her. She slipped away, ducking out of and under his arms so efficiently, he could only stare after her.

He shook his head and sauntered to the couch, dropping heavily onto the plump cushions. He sprawled out, his feet on the floor and his legs crossed at the ankles. One muscular arm behind his head completed the picture of an entirely relaxed man. He glanced up at Melody, smiling lazily. He reached out to her, but she ignored him and moved to the recliner on the other side of the room.

Mary's old tabby cat, Millie, lay curled up in a tight ball on the tattered recliner. Melody reached out to move her, but Chase spoke. "I wouldn't do that if I were you."

"Why not?" she asked.

"Old Millie's a tiger when it comes to her chair. I suggest you leave her alone."

Was he kidding? She couldn't be sure. She met his gaze, attempting to read him, but she couldn't. She turned back to the old cat, who promptly hissed and swiped at her with a fast and furious paw.

"See?" Chase intoned with a wince. "Did she get you?"

Melody shook her head and crossed the room. Chase reached for her hand again. She dodged him and took a seat on the couch, albeit at the other end. Chase patted the space beside him. "Sit by me. What's the fun of sitting all the way down there? You're practically a continent away. Join me on the west coast, Melody." His eyes were alight with laughter, and Melody chuckled.

She realized she and Chase were playing a cat-and-mouse game of their own, and, she had to admit, she was enjoying herself. When she let her guard down for a second, Chase took the opportunity to seize her arm and gently haul her over to him. She gasped and found herself pressed against him, tucked into the crook of his arm.

"This is much nicer," he said with a chuckle.

She smiled into his eyes. "You're right. It is."

"Are you free tomorrow evening?" Chase asked with a hopeful gleam in his eye.

She nodded, thinking she was relieved that the next day was Friday and that she hadn't signed on for additional overtime hours.

"Would you go out with me?" he asked. "Saturday night too?"

She nodded again, smiling. It looked as if her social schedule suddenly rivaled her father's.

Chapter Eleven

Two weeks later, the night of the school dance, Melody arrived home from work a couple of hours late. A glance at the wall clock in the kitchen confirmed that there was no sense in her changing out of her uniform, since she would need to leave in an hour. Her father was watching TV in the living room, and she quickly fixed herself a peanut butter sandwich. She grabbed a banana and a Diet Coke from the fridge and then joined her father in front of the TV.

"Hey, Mel," he said. "Good day?" Before she could answer, he turned back to the TV, and she felt relieved. She didn't feel much like talking.

She started when the phone rang. She rose to answer it in the kitchen.

"Hello, Melody," Chase said cheerfully. "Looking forward to tonight?"

Melody considered her answer to his question but figured honesty was the best policy. "In a word, no."

He feigned surprise at the end of the phone line. "Melody, surely you're happy to do your part to keep our young people on track. You may very well make a difference in a young person's life tonight."

"Is that what I'm doing?" she asked. "And I thought I was going there to help you kick butt and take names."

Chase was apparently speechless. But finally she heard his deep, throaty chuckle. "You know, Melody, I'm starting to see that you have a real propensity for violence."

"Which is why I wanted to work at the motocross tonight," she said pointedly.

"My dad mentioned that the motocross can be dangerous. He said people often get belligerent."

"And your point is . . . ?"

"You could get hurt," he said evenly.

"I can take care of myself, Chase."

"I'm well aware of that, Melody. God knows, you've demonstrated it time and again. It's just . . ."

"What?"

"Nothing," he said crossly. "I'll see you tonight."

She sensed he was upset, though she didn't know why. So her job could be dangerous. What of it? She was well-trained and capable.

Later, as she drove to the high school, she revisited

her earlier conversation with Chase. Obviously he was concerned about her safety. On some level, she understood, since she was beginning to think Chase might have feelings for her. How did she feel about that?

She found herself thinking more and more about him, even while on the job, and she found that curious and slightly disturbing. She knew it was critical that she retain her focus when she was working, since letting her guard down could mean the difference between life and death for herself or someone else.

With a frustrated shake of her head, Melody made a decision not to think about Chase right now—to get her mind on to the business at hand. Or rather, on to the high school dance at hand.

Melody parked her patrol car and headed into the school, making a beeline for the office when she spied her friend Jill there. She approached the receptionist with a rueful smile. "You're working late, Jill."

"I'm chaperoning the dance," her friend told her. "Thought I might score some brownie points with Principal Carter." She grinned wickedly, and Melody smiled uncertainly.

Did Jill have feelings for Chase? Really have feelings? Melody felt a stab of displeasure, and her eyes widened at the realization. *Oh, my goodness,* she realized, the green-eyed monster had reared its ugly head.

That wasn't like her, she knew, but she couldn't deny feeling a spike of jealousy when her friend mentioned wanting to score points with Chase. *Hmm*. What did that mean, she wondered. Really mean?

Maybe she was—gulp—beginning to fall for him? Or had she loved him all along? That was ridiculous, she told herself. He'd only just returned home after years away. She wondered, were old memories clouding her judgment? She and Chase had grown up together—maybe their shared histories accounted for her confused feelings. Maybe nostalgia had colored her thinking. She sighed loudly, and Jill shot a questioning glance her way.

"Are you all right, Melody?"

"Oh, I'm fine. I just wish I was at the motocross instead of here," she said, diverting the conversation away from Chase and her troublesome thoughts about him.

"Well, we're glad you're here. It should be a fun night." The masculine voice startled her, and she spun around.

Chase eyed her lazily, his brown eyes seeming to take her in from the top of her head to the tips of her toes. She colored under his scrutiny.

Jill glanced from Chase to Melody, seeming to realize in an instant that any attempts she made to attract Chase's attention would be futile. The man clearly had a thing for Melody.

"I think I'll get over to the gym," Jill said, attempting a smile. "See you both later."

Chase nodded, but his eyes remained fixed on Melody.

"You know, Chase," she said, "I'm here to do a job, not to have a good time."

He raked a hand through his hair. "I'm hoping you don't have to do much policing tonight," he said with a sad smile. "If we have any more trouble, the school board is likely to nix upcoming dances."

"I'm sorry to hear that," Melody said, for lack of something better to say. The fact was, in her view, if the kids couldn't conduct themselves properly and abide by both the laws of the school and the community, then perhaps they didn't deserve future dances.

Chase watched her, seeming to read her thoughts. "Melody, things aren't always black-and-white. There are some very gray issues on the subject of school dances and the kids who look forward to them. In fact, there are many, many good kids here," he told her. "Although, I understand how your perception could be skewed by the work you do day in and day out. I imagine police work tends to be black-and-white."

Melody furrowed her brow. "What do you mean, Chase?"

"You've either broken the law, or you haven't."

"It isn't *that* simple," Melody protested. "And my perception isn't *skewed,*" she added in a shrill voice.

"Melody, I can read you like a book. Maybe it's having grown up together, or maybe it's because . . ."

Melody raised a hand to silence him. She really didn't want to get into this now. This was not the time or the place. She had work to do.

Chase took a step closer to her, his eyes boring into hers. He started to speak again, but another police officer entered the office. Melody and Chase turned in unison.

Melody quickly introduced Chase to Andy Benton, a co-worker on the day shift. Close to her age, Andy was a good cop, and Melody liked him quite a lot. Fair-haired, freckled, and boasting a slight build, Andy was a man of few words who had actually found his voice when he'd asked her out several times.

She had gone out with him a couple of times but had realized that dating a co-worker was rife with potential problems. She had said as much to him, and while he had accepted her decision, he hadn't liked it. Every once in a while she caught him watching her with unconcealed interest.

Chase extended a hand to Andy. "Good to meet you, Officer Benton."

"You too," the man said. "Where would you like Melody and me to be? Do you want us in the parking lot or inside the gym?"

"If you could patrol inside and outside, including the gym and the parking lot, that would be great," Chase told him. "Also, the kids tend to go down to the stadium, which they are *not* supposed to do. Should you find anyone there, it's grounds for immediate expulsion from the dance, as is any sign of drugs or alcohol on a student. Drugs or alcohol warrants a call to parents, and that's also where you both come in. I guess you do what you have to do. If a physical fight breaks out, parties involved are to be escorted to the office while parents are called. Verbal clashes are handled by me." He thought for a moment. "I guess that's it. I'm hoping things go smoothly tonight," he added.

Andy nodded and turned to Melody. "Ready to go?"

She glanced at Chase, nodded, and then followed Andy out of the room.

The twosome began their patrol of the parking lot, insuring that the kids exited their vehicles and headed directly for the gym. Any teens appearing to consider a detour were given the option to enter the school or leave. Melody actually found herself enjoying interacting with the kids, all of whom knew her from seeing her on the job. She responded to them, often with gentle teasing, and most seemed like good kids.

Once the two officers directed the students inside, Jill waited at the entry doors, keeping a keen eye open and directing students to the gym.

Any sign of suspicious activity was dealt with expediently, and all in all, Melody had to admit that things were going well. She had just commented as much to Andy when Chase walked over to them, seemingly pleased as well with how the event was going.

"Everything all right out here?" he asked. He glanced from Melody to Andy, who happened to be in the parking lot together. He gave Andy a short, speculative glance—his eyes narrowed slightly—and Melody didn't miss the action.

"Would you mind staying out here and keeping an eye on the lot?" Chase asked Andy. "We've had problems with car prowls in the past, among other things," he admitted.

Andy nodded, and Chase turned to Melody. "If you could patrol the halls for a while, that would be great. All the classrooms should be dark, but if you happen to see a light on, let me know. It's a sign of somebody doing something he or she shouldn't be."

Melody started inside, and Chase fell into step beside her. He surprised her when he spoke. "You and Andy seem to be pretty good friends."

She nodded. She'd heard something in his voice, and she refused to acknowledge it or respond to it. Was Chase jealous? That was ridiculous. But then, she couldn't deny she had been jealous earlier. *Good grief.*

"We are. He's a good officer," she said succinctly.

"All right, then, I'll check out the hallways. See you."

He remained beside her, much to her chagrin, until she stopped and pinned him with a stare. "I have a job to do, Chase. Remember?"

He in turn measured her with a look. "Be careful."

She resisted the urge to thump him upside his head. "Chase, I can take care of myself. You know that. You suddenly seem unwilling to accept that. Why?"

He didn't respond immediately but glanced at the ground and then back up, and he snared her gaze. "I know you can take care of yourself, Melody. It's just that I worry about you. Sometimes I still think of you as that little towheaded kid who used to follow me everywhere, and I get protective, and then, at other times, I definitely see you as the woman you've become. Trust me, *I see you* . . ."

"Okay, okay." Melody raised a hand to silence him. This was definitely a conversation better left for later. "Chase, if you could just leave me to do my job, I'll be fine." She strode off, leaving him to his thoughts.

She made a quick check of the hallways, finding them empty of students. The classrooms were clear as well. It wasn't until she arrived at a glass display case in the main hall leading to the gym that she encountered trouble.

Melody approached two boys who were apparently involved in a heated argument that had all the earmarks of escalating. One boy moved around nervously, shifting his feet, staring at the other boy with venom. The second boy, tall and solidly built, stood his ground.

She had hoped to avoid any kind of altercation tonight. She strode over to the twosome, who were quickly being surrounded by a swelling group of onlookers.

"What's the trouble, boys?" Melody asked lazily as she approached the teens. She pushed her way through the group. "There's nothing to see here," she told the crowd. "Back to the gym, everybody."

With a collective groan, the group dispersed, but the two boys remained locked in a form of visual mortal combat. The two had angry eyes fastened on each other, and neither seemed willing to walk away.

Melody reached toward the smaller boy and gently took his arm. He jerked his arm away, turning on her with a cold fury.

"You need to settle down," she said in a firm voice, "or you're going to have to leave."

"I don't have to do anything," he said.

Melody only smiled slightly. She would not be intimidated by a child. She turned toward the bigger boy. "You need to go into the gym right now, or you'll need to leave the school."

"And what if I don't wanna leave?" he asked, watching her menacingly.

"Then I'll arrest you," Melody said simply.

"I'd like to see you try," the boy said, taking a step toward her. "I'll make you sorry, lady."

Melody's senses were tingling with anticipation, quick and alert. She could easily handle this kid, though he had no idea just how easily. She wasn't given the opportunity to, because suddenly Chase had a hold of the front of the boy's shirt. He yanked the boy toward him, only to slam him against a nearby locker. He pinned the boy with angry eyes. "You *ever* talk to her that way again, you're the one who'll be sorry. Now, you get out of here, or I will have you arrested."

The boy skulked off, and Chase turned to the smaller boy. "What's it gonna be? Are you staying or going?"

"Staying," the boy said sheepishly, and he shuffled into the gym.

Chase turned to Melody. "Are you all right?"

She was so furious with him for intervening while she had been doing her job, she simply couldn't find words. How dare he treat her as if she were some kind of helpless female? She could fight her own battles.

When she finally found her voice, she turned on him. "How . . . dare . . . you do that?" she hissed.

"What?" he asked, eyes wide and bewildered.

"How dare you interfere with my job?"

"I . . ."

She silenced him with a hostile glance. "Why did you want law enforcement on-site, Chase, if you weren't prepared to let us do our jobs?"

Chase raked a hand through his hair, seeming to search for the right words to soothe her but suspecting there were none. He had interfered, but he hadn't been able to stop himself. What if one of the boys had harmed her? It would have killed him.

"Melody, listen. I'm sorry. I wasn't thinking."

"No, you weren't," she said softly, and she spun on her heel and left for the parking lot.

As she stepped into the night air, she tipped her face to the breeze. She was still furious with Chase. How dare he intervene in police business and compromise her authority? Heck, she ought to arrest *him*. She could have handled the boy fine on her own.

"He has feelings for you."

Melody spun around. Jill watched her with a slight, knowing smile. "It's obvious the man loves you."

Melody chortled. Chase didn't love her. He didn't even know her anymore. She shook her head ruefully. "I don't think so. We're . . ."

Jill laid a soft hand on her forearm. "He loves you, all right. I have to go back in. You be careful out here, Mel."

Melody hugged herself and then abruptly dropped her arms. It was hardly the posture of a rough-and-ready law enforcement officer. She glanced at her watch. It was nearing ten, and, thankfully, the dance ended at eleven. The hour couldn't come soon enough for her.

After a quick perusal of the parking lot and after directing a wayward couple back to the gym, Melody entered the school again. She found herself back at the display case, surveying the assortment of trophies and plaques commemorating various students and sports teams over the years. She spied her own name several times.

She'd won countless citizenship awards, had been captain of the girls' basketball team, and had been a star on the math team, having led her team to first place at a statewide competition.

"You were definitely an overachiever," Chase commented, and she could hear the contrition in his voice.

Melody turned to meet his troubled gaze. "I . . . am . . . so . . . angry with you," she said truthfully. "I've never met anyone so threatened by my job."

Chase gave her a startled glance. "Melody, it's not that!" he insisted. "It has nothing to do with being threatened. It has to do with being . . . scared. I . . . uh . . ." He raked a hand through his hair. "Melody, I guess I lost my head. No, I know I lost my head. The kid threatened you, and my first inclination was to protect you."

Melody extended a hand to him. "I'm Melody. Apparently we haven't met before. Good grief, Chase, you of all people know I can handle myself just fine. I do not need you or anyone 'protecting' me."

He pinned her with his eyes. "Melody, I know that. It was a knee-jerk reaction. I . . ."

"You what, Chase?" she said tiredly.

"I, uh, have feelings for you." Suddenly his eyes widened, as if he'd just made an alarming discovery. "Melody, I love you."

Melody's jaw dropped. She couldn't even respond. Those words were certainly the last she'd expected to hear from him tonight, for Pete's sake. Not here, at the school, while she was on the job.

On one hand, she wanted to kill him, and on the other, she wanted to wrap her arms around his neck and kiss him. "Chase . . ." She shook her head and sighed. "We can't . . . talk about this now." She hurried away.

A cool burst of air rushed over her as she tossed open the double doors at the front of the school. She jogged out to the edge of the parking lot, where she remained until the dance ended.

Chapter Twelve

Melody found her father up and at the kitchen table when she arrived home close to midnight. She was surprised to see him there but soon discovered he had been waiting up for her.

"How was the dance?" he asked.

She gave a dramatic shudder. "Brought back memories, Pop. Made me remember why I preferred riding my horse to hanging out at the school after hours. But, I have to admit, many of the kids were great."

Tank smiled faintly. "How's Chase?"

"Aggravating," she muttered softly.

Tank gave her a curious look. "You know, Ed tells me he believes that Chase has fallen pretty hard for you."

"Pop, he told me he loves me tonight—while I was

149

on the job," she said with a frustrated shake of her head. "Pop, he . . . he hardly knows me."

Tank cocked his head to one side, studying his daughter. "Honey, Chase knows you. He's known you since the day you were born. He was five years old when we brought you home from the hospital. He was so excited to see you, waiting at our house with Ed. And you know what? That very day he announced he was going to marry you when you grew up."

"Pop, nobody ever told me that before."

"I never thought much about it," he said. "Fact is, nobody thought Chase would ever come back to Trentonburg and settle down. I'll tell you what, though. It's clear to everybody who sees the way Chase looks at you, he loves you."

"Pop, the man makes me crazy sometimes."

"Your mama used to make me crazy," he said with a grin.

Their eyes locked for a brief moment, until Tank glanced away, swiping at his eyes.

"What's wrong, Pop?"

He shook his head. "You know, I'm enjoying Lucy's company so much, but then, sometimes, it feels so wrong—as if it's traitorous to even consider dating anyone else."

"Pop, Mom would want you to be happy," she said softly, reaching across the table to pat his arm.

"Oh, honey, I know. And she would want you to be happy too."

"I am happy."

"Are you? Melody, have you really thought about what you want from life? Do you want to be married someday?"

"Well, yes, someday."

"It sure doesn't seem like it to me. Every time a guy gets close to you, you hightail it to the hills—in your case, 'hills' meaning work. Work is your be-all, Melody, which is fine if it's what you really want."

"Lately I don't know what I want, Pop," she said miserably.

"Do you have feelings for Chase? Seems to me like you do."

Melody smiled awkwardly. "This is kind of embarrassing to be discussing with my father," she admitted.

"Go on, honey. It's okay."

"I'm . . . attracted to him, and I do like him. . . . I might even love him." She moaned. "But I do know one thing: he has a real problem with my occupation. Pop, he actually interfered with my doing my job tonight, if you can believe that."

"What happened?"

"I was breaking up a fight between two kids, and Chase jumped in."

"So?"

Melody pressed her eyelids closed and counted to three before snaring her father's gaze. "Why do men always want to view me as some sort of helpless female?"

"Chase doesn't see you that way, Melody. I don't either."

"Oh, you do too. You'd like nothing better than to see me in the role of wife and mother, forgoing any kind of career."

"I would not! You've worked too hard to give up your career. I do think you work too much, and if you'd actually work your assigned shift, without giving away your time as if it isn't at a premium—which it is—then you'd have time for, say, Chase in your life. But if not Chase, someone else. Or, heck, Mel, no one else, if that's your choice. But, *do not* give every bit of yourself to this department or any other. Because in the end, it's a thing, Mel, impersonal and uncaring, and it can't give you any kind of real return on your investment."

Melody rose from the table and filled a glass with water before rejoining her father. Deep in thought, she stared at the crystalline water. She shot a furtive glance at her father. She had never heard him talk about the department that way before. He sounded embittered, almost angry, and she wondered why.

Hesitantly, she posed a question. "Pop, what's going on with you? You used to love the job. You still do."

He swiped at his eyes. "I loved your mother more, but it took her dying for me to see it." Suddenly tears flowed freely from her father's eyes, and Melody reached for his hand.

"Pop, Mom knew how much you loved her," she said softly.

He sniffled and wiped at his eyes with a shirtsleeve. "I know she did. I know."

"And, Pop, Mom did understand the demands of the job. She really did, and she was proud of the work you did."

"I know that too," Tank said, and he cleared his throat. "I just wish sometimes I could go back in time. I don't ever want you feeling like that. No regrets, Mel. You don't want regrets."

"I have to live my life."

"Yes, yes, you do." He was silent for a moment, gathering his thoughts. Finally he posed a question. "Melody, think about the men you've dated in the past. Did they have issues with your being a police officer?"

"You mean besides the guy who turned out to be a serial burglar?" she teased in a droll voice.

"Melody," he said sternly, but he chuckled slightly.

"Oh, I don't know, Pop. Some seemed okay with it; others didn't. It didn't matter to me one way or the other."

"Because you didn't love them. They didn't and couldn't influence you because you didn't have the depth of feelings for them that you have for Chase."

Melody paused, thinking. "Okay, Pop, I admit I—"

"You love him," Tank cut in succinctly.

Melody smiled softly. "Yeah, okay, I do, but he shouldn't have interfered with my doing my job to-night. I know my work bothers him—and that bothers me!"

Tank furrowed his brow. "Melody, to be honest, I doubt Chase has a problem with your job. But let's say he does. Put yourself in Chase's shoes. Just suppose his feelings for you are real, and he's only recently discovered those feelings. Imagine how scared he must be, falling for somebody who puts her life on the line every time she goes out the door."

"When you put it like that, maybe it's not fair for a cop to marry at all—or have any kind of relationship, for that matter."

"You should have been a lawyer," Tank said in a frustrated voice.

"Did Mom have a problem with your decision to go into law enforcement?" Melody asked, watching him intently.

Tank raked a hand through his hair. "I believe she did, though she made the best of it. Besides, it's different when a man . . ."

Melody gasped. Was her father really going to say what she thought he might? "Go on, Pop," she prompted, ready to pounce.

"You're not going to like this, but, when you come right down to it, historically men have dominated the field of law enforcement. In recent years women have begun entering the profession, and they do great, but the stakes are different for women."

Melody gasped. "They are not."

He nodded fiercely. "They are. Suppose you have a

wagonload of kids, and then you go out and someone kills you. Someone just cost your children their mother."

"Yeah, and you could just as easily have been killed on the job."

"Yes, but it's different, Melody," he persisted. "Whether you like it or not, it's different. Kids need a mother—a father too, in a perfect world, but . . ."

Melody was aghast. "I don't agree with you, Pop. I really don't, and I'm not about to give up my job for anyone. Plenty of women officers manage to have families and do just fine."

"Yes, Melody, because they actually clock out after their prescribed workday. They don't put in eighteen hours, only to start over the next day, and then tack on another overtime shift. Melody, you're working yourself to death. Honey, life is about balance, about thinking about yourself sometimes. Don't you realize that by putting yourself out there, making five traffic stops to other cops' one, or taking three calls to other officers' one, the odds are *you're* going to get citizen complaints, or you're going to get so worn out, you'll let your guard down? I don't want to see that happen."

"Since when is a work ethic a bad thing?" Melody muttered testily. "I learned it from you."

"Okay, Melody, I'm just calling it like I see it. Besides, I don't think Chase would ever ask you to give up anything important to you. Chase loves you, that's what I see, and the truth is, he's a good kid. Always was. A bit of a prankster, but a good kid. And he's definitely grown into a good man. So he worries about you. So sue him. He's likely trying to sort through all the things a person deals with when they love a cop. My advice to you, cut him some slack. Give him time. Lord knows, you're great at giving away your time," he finished with a frustrated shake of his head. "And you're right, you learned it from me," he finished with a self-deprecating laugh.

Tank awkwardly rose from the table, dropped into the wheelchair, and rolled away.

Melody rose early the next morning, since she had volunteered for an overtime shift. As she dressed for her day, she realized that maybe her father was right. She didn't have personal boundaries when it came to work. She hadn't needed to take another overtime shift—she didn't need the money—but she had felt compelled to take it. She knew she worked harder and longer than almost anyone else at the department, but she couldn't help herself. She had been cut from the same cloth as her father, and perhaps she had something to prove—though she couldn't be sure what that something was or to whom she thought she had to prove it. Her father, perhaps? She just didn't know.

"Lucy's coming, right?" she asked him as she stepped into the kitchen. She made a beeline for the percolator and poured hot coffee into a travel mug.

Tank glanced up. "Uh, yeah, she's coming." He

watched Melody uncertainly. "Mel, I want to apologize for last night. I probably said more than I should have."

"No, Pop, it's all right. One thing we do well is communicate. I'm told that's a good thing."

"Dr. Phil says so," Tank said with a grin.

Melody chuckled. She'd been surprised recently to discover that her father and Lucy watched the TV personality together each day, like clockwork. "But my guess is," Tank said, "you didn't like a lot of what I had to say."

"Since when has that ever stopped you?" Melody said with a sparkle of humor in her eyes. "Besides, you made some valid points." She spread her arms. "Look at me. I'm off to work on a Saturday, when I could have had a day off."

"Old habits die hard," Tank said with a sad smile. "You be careful out there today."

"Always," she said.

Melody left the house and was climbing into her squad car when Chase drove up. She was surprised to see him so early, since it was barely after six o'clock. He parked and dropped down out of his truck.

Melody noticed he was dressed in well-worn jeans that hugged his muscular thighs, and he wore a T-shirt with the high school mascot emblazoned across the front. When he approached, his brown eyes fixed on her face, she saw that his features were drawn tight.

"Hello, Melody."

"You're up awfully early," she commented.

He nodded. "Yeah, I was hoping you'd be up too, and you haven't disappointed me. You're working." It was a statement, not a question.

"I took an overtime shift."

"I was hoping we could talk, Melody. I feel terrible about last night."

Melody checked her watch. "Look, Chase, I really have to move. I need to put myself into service by six-fifteen."

He nodded crisply. "I'll be working out at my property today. If you get a free minute, do you think you could stop by? If you call first, I can run into town and pick up lunch for us."

Melody winced. "It's hard to say if I'll make it out your way," she answered honestly. "There's no predicting my call load."

"I understand." He smiled tightly. "I'm telling myself it's a good sign you're actually speaking to me."

"Frankly, Chase, you sort of left me speechless last night."

"I know." He shook his head ruefully. "Telling you I love you in front of the display case at the high school wasn't exactly how I imagined declaring my feelings for you—to you," he added. "We really need to talk."

"Chase, to be honest with you, I'm pretty riled up about your stepping in when I was dealing with those boys."

"I know. You have a right to be, but, Melody, if you

hadn't been there, I would have been forced to handle them myself anyway, and, had the boy gotten mouthy with me, I probably would have grabbed a hold of him just like I did last night." He shook his head. "You know, Melody, as wild and woolly as I was as a kid, I *never* would have spoken to a police officer the way that kid talked to you. That level of disrespect astounds me, and—"

"Chase," she cut in, "first, I *was* there. Second, how he talked to me was my problem, not yours. Bottom line, I had a job to do, and you interfered."

"Is there anything I can say or do that will convince you that I get that I crossed the line? I was up half the night thinking about it—about us. I'm hoping you're still willing to give 'us' a chance."

He watched her with imploring eyes, and Melody sighed, realizing she needed to get on the road. "Can we talk later? I really do have to go."

"Absolutely. You know where I'll be."

Melody climbed into her patrol car, put herself into service, and drove off. She spied Chase in her rearview mirror. He watched her departure for a few seconds, and then she saw him climb the steps to her front door. Apparently he intended to visit with her father, and she was glad Tank would have company for a while until Lucy arrived.

Chapter Thirteen

Melody hadn't spoken to Chase since the morning after the dance. She hadn't had an opportunity to speak to him Saturday, since she hadn't found any breaks in her schedule to stop by his property. Then, at the end of her overtime shift Saturday, she had pulled over a man who had several warrants, and she'd ended up staying at work until late evening, processing the guy and completing the incident report.

When she finally arrived home, Tank told her Chase had called, but it was too late to return his call. She didn't see or hear from him Sunday, and Lucy mentioned he had gone out of town for the day for some school-related event.

As she drove toward home Monday, having decided to both check on her dad and grab a quick lunch, she remembered her conversation with her father after she'd arrived home from the dance.

Tank had made some valid points. She hadn't actually ever put herself in the shoes of someone either in or about to embark on a relationship with someone in law enforcement. It couldn't be easy loving a police officer—and for so many reasons. Besides the obvious dangers involved in the profession, there were the long hours and the fact that the job could be so demanding both physically and mentally. It could be emotionally devastating as well.

Police officers saw things on the job that the rest of the population would never see. They were first to arrive on the scene at some of the most horrendous acts of physical violence perpetrated by humans against one another. Often they saw injured children, or worse. It did take a toll, and Melody knew that many law enforcement marriages ended in divorce. The statistics weren't promising.

Melody had to admit to herself, she didn't often speak about the things she saw and did on the job. She had walked into scenes that made her stomach turn. Early in her career, she had even left a crime scene in tears once, but she had never allowed herself to cry again. She had a job to do and could not be effective in it were she prone to breaking down. Mental toughness was critical.

She tried to remember—had her father spoken about his work at home? She couldn't recall, but then she remembered that occasionally he had spoken to her mother in hushed whispers, which usually meant her mom would soon be talking to her about some peril or someone in the community to watch out for.

To date, she just hadn't given much thought to the toll of her job on the people around her. She wasn't sure she wanted to. She did remember that her mother had cried when she told her she planned to follow in Tank's footsteps. But then her mother had rallied and had been nothing but supportive thereafter. Most likely, she realized, Melody would not be deterred, so she had made the best of it. Spouses, children, and parents of law enforcement officers were adept at "making the best of it."

Melody steered her car down the gravel lane and parked in front of the house. She saw Lucy's car parked nearby. In the house, she found the twosome sitting at the kitchen table sharing lunch. She couldn't miss the huge bouquet of white roses on a nearby countertop and moved closer to smell one particularly lovely bud.

Melody grinned at her father as she dropped into a chair beside him. "Well, aren't you the Romeo?" she declared.

Her father reddened—not because he'd purchased the roses, but because he hadn't. If only he had thought to get Lucy roses. She had seemed to love them when the deliveryman brought them to the front door.

"They're for you," her father said curtly.

Melody raised a surprised eyebrow. She stood and moved to check out the card. It read simply: *I hope we can talk soon. Chase.*

"They're beautiful, aren't they?" Lucy said. "I believe Chase has fallen for you, my dear."

Melody smiled at Lucy but didn't respond. She wasn't sure what to say. Quickly she assembled a ham sandwich and grabbed a Diet Coke. "See you both," she called, and then she strode to her car.

So, Chase had sent her roses. She loved roses, especially the gorgeous white roses he'd chosen. But if he thought the roses would assuage her feeling about the other night, he was mistaken. It would take more than a bouquet for her to forgive Chase's interference in her job. She suspected he knew that.

Melody drove back toward Trentonburg, unaware that Chase pulled down her lane shortly after. He parked in front of the house and climbed the porch steps. Lucy answered the door, and he followed her into the kitchen and dropped into a chair, spying the roses immediately.

"Has she seen them yet?" he asked no one in particular, tapping his fingers nervously on the tabletop.

"Why, yes, dear," Lucy responded. "Melody just left. You only missed her by a moment or two."

"Did she . . . seem to like the roses?"

"How could she not, dear?" Lucy said, smiling fondly at her nephew.

"She was angry with me Friday night," he said with a wince, "and I can't blame her. I messed up," he admitted. He raked a hand through his hair. "I blew it, and I wish I knew what to do to make things right."

Tank sat up straight. "Candy," he said crisply. "Chocolate oughta do the trick."

"Candy? I don't want Melody thinking I'm trying to buy her forgiveness," Chase muttered uncertainly. "But you think she'd like chocolates better than the roses?" he inquired worriedly.

"Truth is, Chase, my Melody's a practical gal," Tank said. "Unless the roses have a root-ball and she can plant 'em in the soil, she isn't likely to be overly impressed."

Chase slouched in the chair. "Really? I thought all women loved flowers."

"Well, most do," Lucy said, watching Tank with a frown. From her vantage point, Melody had seemed to like the roses, root-ball or no root-ball.

"What kind of chocolates?" Chase inquired with interest. "Does she have a favorite brand?"

"Anything chocolate," Tank said with certainty.

Lucy spoke up, suggesting a particular variety.

"Oh, okay," Chase said, "that helps. You think she'd like them, then?"

Lucy patted his hand. "I know she would, dear."

"You could get Melody a pack of M&M's and she'd be delighted," Tank chortled. "No need for anything too fancy."

Chase glanced at Lucy uncertainly.

"I'd go with boxed chocolates," she suggested sweetly, and then she turned toward Tank and watched him as if he were a space alien.

Tank noticed and shifted uncomfortably. Had he said or done something wrong? He'd have to chew on it later, since Chase posed another question.

"Tank, you think Melody'll ever give me the time of day again? She wanted to shoot me the other night. I really don't blame her."

"I don't blame her either," Lucy said softly, and Tank shot her a surprised glance.

"Lucy!" Tank said, aghast. "Chase came here for advice—for a pep talk. He didn't mean any harm the other night." Tank turned his attention to Chase. "Truth is, Chase, Melody can get mighty riled up. But between you and me, son, I gave her an earful the other night. May have even made her see some sense. No need to thank me."

Chase gulped loudly. Tank's talking to Melody on his behalf couldn't possibly be good. "I . . . I appreciate that, Tank," he said doubtfully, glancing at his aunt.

She smiled serenely. "Things will work out, Chase. You just be yourself, and things should fall into place. I know Melody will understand that you meant no harm. But just don't make the same mistake twice," she said, wagging a warning finger at him.

Tank chuckled and reached forward to thump Chase

on the back. "You're a good man, Chase. I was telling Melody the other night how when we brought her home from the hospital as a newborn, you and Ed were waiting here at the house. Your ma was at the hospital with us. Anyway, you took one look at my little Melody and said you were gonna marry that girl someday."

Chase smiled. "So I actually proposed to her long before she proposed to me," he said in wonderment.

"It's meant to be," Tank said with certainty. "It's meant to be."

When Melody arrived home from work that night, miraculously on time, she spied Chase sitting on the porch swing even as she parked her patrol car. She climbed the stairs slowly.

Immediately she spied the box of chocolates in his hand. And was that a rosebush he was holding? She narrowed her eyes and realized, yes, it was a rosebush.

"Hello, Melody." Chase rose from the swing and passed the chocolates and rosebush to her simultaneously. "These are for you."

Melody took the items, her brow furrowing into a frown. "Thanks, I love chocolates." She eyed the rosebush. "And rose . . . bushes."

He nodded his head up and down, as if he'd gotten something right. He pointed to the base of the plant. "Look . . . a root-ball."

Melody saw that, indeed, the bush had a roof-ball. She eyed it, curious, and then glanced away, feeling self-conscious and unsure. Chase seemed awfully pleased with that root-ball.

Chase spoke up, enlightening her as to why. "Your dad told me you don't especially care for cut flowers but prefer a plant with a root-ball. I'm sorry. Had I known, I wouldn't have bothered you with the roses earlier."

" 'Bothered' . . . ?" Melody's mouth dropped open. *"What?"*

Chase frowned then, watching her uncertainly. "Uh, well, Tank said you're a practical woman and prefer to plant your own flowers rather than receive cut flowers."

"Oh, right," Melody said sarcastically, "I just *abhor* cut flowers. *Pop!*"

Chase watched her retreating figure, brow furrowed in a deep frown. "Am I glad I didn't bring her a bag of M&M's," he muttered to himself as he followed her into the house and into the kitchen.

"Pop, did you tell Chase I don't like fresh flowers?" she demanded.

Tank glanced at Melody with alarm, then at Chase. He shot the younger man a dirty look.

"Don't you be giving Chase an angry look," Melody commanded. "Telling him I don't like fresh flowers! What woman doesn't love flowers, especially roses?"

Lucy, who sat nearby, nodded her head in agreement.

"Well, I'm sorry, Melody," Tank said. "I thought I was helping. Your mother didn't like fresh flowers."

"Of course, she did! It was you who didn't like fresh flowers. You said they were a waste of money!"

Tank gulped loudly. Maybe it *was* he who preferred that his plants come with a root-ball. "I'm sorry, Chase," Tank said. "I guess I steered you wrong, boy." Tank ventured a glance at Lucy. She smiled benignly, but he figured it was taking a good deal of self-control for her to maintain that neutral face. She probably wanted flowers too, and not anything with a root-ball either.

Melody turned to Chase. "Will you give me a minute to change out of my uniform? You and I do need to talk."

He nodded and sat down at the table to wait. Tank shot him another dirty look. "Couldn't keep your dog-gone mouth shut, could you, boy?"

Chase opened his mouth to speak, laughed instead, and then clamped his mouth shut. Melody was apparently willing to speak to him, and he hoped to remain on her good side. If it meant Tank's being the object of her wrath, then so be it. Besides, the man *had* steered him wrong.

When Melody entered the kitchen, dressed in denim shorts and a soft pink T-shirt, Chase was hard-pressed to keep his eyes off her. Dainty and petite, she had curves in all the right places.

"Chase, you want to come outside with me?" she asked.

He nodded and followed her to the small barn. "What are you doing?" he asked with interest.

"I'm looking for a shovel," she informed. "I need to plant this . . . root-ball," she said, eyeing the bush ruefully.

"You do?"

"Well, yeah. I can't have the rosebush dying. Besides, every time I look at it, I'll remember it was my first gift with a root-ball," she said with a chuckle.

"And you'll likely also remember what a moron I can be," Chase said with chagrin. He stared into her face and reached to brush a tendril of hair from her cheek. "Melody, the other night, my emotions got in the way of good judgment, and I promise I'll do my best never to let it happen again. I'm not saying it'll be easy, but I'll do my best."

She nodded. "I appreciate that, Chase."

"Can we start fresh?" he asked hopefully.

Melody nodded tentatively. She wondered, was Chase ready for a relationship with a cop? And, perhaps more to the point, if she truly searched her heart and soul, was she ready for a relationship with him?

"We can start fresh," Melody said finally.

"I'm glad," he murmured, pulling her close again and kissing the top of her head. She felt his warm breath against her hair when he spoke again. "We need to talk more. After we plant the bush, will you have dinner with me?"

"Burger Barn?" Melody suggested hopefully. She was starving for a big, juicy burger and a strawberry shake.

"Anything you like."

"Now, those are words any woman likes to hear."

Sitting across from Chase at the Burger Barn, Melody couldn't help but take in his striking good looks. The man was drop-dead gorgeous, and just like the last time the two had visited the Burger Barn, female patrons watched him with interest.

Interestingly, Chase didn't seem particularly aware of his good looks. He'd joked about being the most eligible bachelor in town, but he never strutted around like many men who were obviously confident in their lady-killing prowess.

Chase reached across the table, taking her hand and meeting her gaze. "Are we good?" he asked. "It's important to me. You're important to me."

Melody nodded. "We're fine," she told him.

Chase smiled into her eyes and was about to say something, when they were interrupted by Commander Manchester.

"Hello, Melody," he said.

She glanced up, smiling. "Oh, hi." She quickly introduced her boss to Chase, who rose and shook the man's hand.

"Good to meet you," Chase said.

"You too. Mind if I join you both for a minute? I'm waiting on a to-go order. I promised Jake if he aced his spelling test, I'd bring home burgers, fries, and shakes. Martha called and told me he got a perfect score. So . . ." He raised a hand, gesturing at his surroundings.

"Well, good for him!" Chase said. "How old is your boy?"

"Ten," Manchester said, smiling fondly before turning to Melody. "Hey, Melody, I wanted to tell you we've completed the investigation on the young kid who hit your dad, and the prosecutor's office intends to file charges."

She nodded. She had suspected as much.

"Will you pass along the information to your dad? And tell him too, I'll be calling him in a week or two to set up a meeting with the prosecuting attorney." He shook his head. "This is a tough one," he admitted. "The boy who hit him is actually a good kid who happened to drink too much on his twenty-first birthday. Although I'm not kidding myself, thinking it's the first time he's ever touched alcohol, it is the first time the kid has ever been in any kind of trouble."

Melody winced, and she couldn't help but wonder when these young college kids were going to realize the seriousness of drinking to excess. Since Trentonburg was a small college town, admittedly there was little to keep the teens and young twenty-somethings occupied when they weren't hitting the books. They often turned to alcohol.

But her loyalty was to her father, and she would never forget the image of him lying on the ground, his leg twisted violently beneath him.

"Well, I should go," Manchester said. "Oh, one more thing. Chase, you apparently approached the school board about installing a police officer at the school in order to keep an eye on things. The truth is, we had already approached them with the idea. Many communities have on-site officers at local schools. Anyway, we're looking into it seriously, and we're wondering if you're available to get together to discuss it next week sometime."

Chase nodded eagerly. "Absolutely."

Manchester nodded at Melody and grinned. "Maybe this one might put in for the job."

Melody felt her cheeks go red. "Ain't gonna happen," she said adamantly.

Manchester chuckled. "Not exciting enough for you, eh, Mel?"

Melody didn't answer but smiled instead. She wouldn't even begin a conversation about the whys. The biggest why was sitting across the booth from her.

Hey! Had Manchester just shot Chase a commiserating glance? She realized he had when the older man stood up and clucked ruefully in her direction.

Were she a man, she doubted Manchester would have behaved that way, and while it grieved her to no end, she could understand it on some level. His wife had been a state trooper and was killed several years before when she was involved in a high-speed chase. The suspects had fled a robbery scene and, during the pursuit, had shot at Manchester's wife, striking her in the shoulder and causing her to veer off the road. She had hit a tree and been killed on impact.

The death had torn the town up, and it had taken a grief-stricken Manchester several years to get over losing his wife. He had only just recently married Martha, a local teacher, and the two seemed happy. Melody was glad and, under the circumstances, was willing to cut the man some slack regarding his protective attitude toward female officers—but only to a point.

"I'll be seeing you both," Manchester said when the girl at the counter called his food order number.

Chase watched the man stride out of the burger joint, and then he turned to Melody. "Is he the man who lost his wife?"

Melody nodded.

"I understand she was a state trooper killed in the line of duty."

Melody nodded again.

Chase met Melody's gaze but seemed to stare right through her. Finally he reached across the table to take her hand again. "Loving a police officer isn't going to be easy," he murmured.

Melody shot him an alarmed glance, and he raised a

quick hand in surrender. "I mean," he clarified, "I know that *you're* more than capable of doing your job. It's just . . ."

"What?" she prompted.

"There are a lot of bad guys out there, but, honey, you don't have to personally take them all out, do you?"

Chapter Fourteen

Tank rolled into the kitchen, almost striking his casted leg on the doorjamb. If he hadn't had his eyes on Lucy, he might have managed to avoid the near-collision, but these days he couldn't seem to keep his eyes off Lucy. She was beautiful, with chestnut brown hair, brown eyes, and those lips. And best of all, she could cook.

Tank glanced at his watch, and Lucy noticed. "Is there anything you need, Tank?"

He shook his head brusquely. The florist had assured him the roses would be delivered before 10:00 A.M., and it was nearly that time. He checked his watch again.

Lucy watched him, curious. "Tank, what's on your mind?"

"Nothing."

He rolled out of the kitchen just as the doorbell rang. He struggled to get to the door before Lucy, which involved some careful maneuvering, considering how his leg jutted out. It just wasn't working out, and he finally gave up, rolling aside to allow Lucy to answer the door.

The deliveryman passed the flowers to her with a grin. She accepted the flowers, closed the door behind her, and followed Tank into the kitchen. Lucy set the gorgeous yellow roses on the countertop, inhaled to enjoy their fragrance, and then moved to sit down at the table.

"Melody will love them," she said, smiling wistfully.

"What makes you think they're for Melody?" Tank demanded gruffly. "Did you look at the card?"

"Well, no," Lucy admitted, rising from her chair and casting Tank a quizzical glance. She walked back to the roses and removed the card. She read it, her eyes widening with pleasure. "Oh, Tank!" She hurried to him and threw her arms around his shoulders. "They're beautiful!" she enthused.

"Well, yeah, of course they are. Woman doesn't even bother checking the card. . . ."

"I won't make that mistake again," she said soothingly, smiling into his eyes and then kissing him lightly on the cheek.

"I have something else for you," he said as he

wheeled himself to a nearby drawer and pulled out a box of chocolates. "I hope you like these. I mean, I imagine you must, since you recommended Chase buy 'em for Melody."

"I love them!" she cried. "Thank you!"

Tank smiled then, a broad, self-satisfied smile. He'd made Lucy happy, all right. And as tempted as he had been to get a hold of a plant with a root-ball, he'd fought the inclination. There was no accounting for what women liked, but he was darned pleased to have gotten it right this time.

Melody was at her desk when a call came in for her from the defense attorney representing the boy who had injured her father. She was surprised by the call. Her father hadn't had any contact with the attorney but wouldn't, normally, since the department was working alongside the prosecutor's office in the handling of the case.

"What can I do for you?" Melody asked coolly, bracing for what was to come.

"I have something for your father," he told her.

"What?" Melody knew she sounded curt, but she couldn't help it.

"Against my advice, the young man who struck your father has written an apology letter. He has asked me repeatedly to arrange a meeting with your dad, but I've advised against it. I can't very well represent him if he doesn't adhere to my advice, but . . ." The man sighed heavily. "He is insistent I get this letter to your father."

"I . . . I can swing by your office to pick it up."

The man gave her directions, and Melody told him she'd be by during her lunch hour. She found herself curious about the letter, though nothing the boy could say to her father would sway her opinion of him. He was a reckless, irresponsible youth who would soon be facing the consequences of his actions.

During the noon hour, Melody picked up the letter from the attorney's office and dropped it onto the passenger seat of her squad car. Her eyes lighted on the sealed envelope often throughout the day, and finally, when she arrived home that night, she passed it to her father.

"What's this?" he asked.

"A letter from the boy who hit you."

Tank seemed taken aback. He didn't speak but studied the envelope as if he had X-ray vision and could see through it. Melody had expected him to open the envelope and begin reading. Instead, he folded it in half and stuffed it into his shirt pocket.

Melody didn't press him to read it, deciding to head upstairs and change out of her work clothes. When she came back downstairs, she found her father still in the kitchen, the letter opened on the tabletop.

"I read it," he said in response to her raised eyebrows.

Melody noted a deep, weary sadness in her father's eyes. "What is it, Pop?"

"He's not a bad kid," he said succinctly. He passed her the letter.

She read it quickly. The boy apologized profusely for his actions, mentioning he had never been drunk before that fateful afternoon. He explained he was an engineering major who was well aware of the dangers of alcohol. Rather than asking Tank to wield his influence to lessen his possible sentence, he admitted his wrongdoing and said he was prepared to pay for his crime. He begged for forgiveness, asked if there was anything he could do to make things right, even offering to help Tank out around the place until he was on his feet again. The boy mentioned he had taken a quarter off from school but didn't specifically say why, although Melody could easily imagine the reason.

Melody laid the letter back on the tabletop.

"What do you think, Melody?" Tank asked.

"What do you mean, 'What do you think?' I think the kid made a terrible error in judgment, and he's going to have to pay for it. What else is there to think?"

Tank shook his head. "I know this kid has never been in any kind of trouble before. This could ruin his life, Melody. If he ends up doing jail time, it'll prevent him from completing his schooling for some time. There's no telling what it'll do to him psychologically."

"Pop, that isn't your problem," Melody said shrilly.

"Your leg may never be the same, thanks to that stupid kid."

Tank watched Melody curiously. "Honey, things aren't always black-and-white. People make mistakes. Heck, baby, I did some mighty stupid things when I was in college too, I'm ashamed to admit. By the grace of God, I didn't end up barreling into someone with my car, but . . . I could have."

Melody gasped, leaning weakly against the chair back. Was her father prepared to allow this kid a pass for what he had done to him? He wasn't getting off that easily—not if she could help it.

"I want to meet with him," Tank said with authority.

"Pop, I don't think—"

Tank raised a hand to silence her. "I want to talk to him, Melody."

Later that night, Chase picked Melody up for a late dinner. He'd had meetings all afternoon but had finally managed to get away. When he arrived at her house, Melody realized he hadn't even had a chance to change out of his work clothes.

"You look tired," she commented, taking in the half circles framing his lower eyelids.

"I am," he admitted.

"Are you sure you're up for dinner?"

"I'll be fine," he said with a yawn.

"Why don't we stop by your folks' so you can change

into something more comfortable, and then why don't we just grab a pizza and eat at my place?"

"I can think of two reasons. Tank. Lucy," he reminded her, as if she needed reminding.

"I meant, we could go to *my* house. I've practically moved back into the little house, except for at night. I still need to be able to hear Pop if he needs me then, but my days and evenings are my own at this point."

"Thanks to Lucy," Chase said.

Melody nodded. "Yep. Thanks to Lucy."

"Ah, to be young and in love," Chase said, and then he arched his eyebrows. "Like us." He reached for her hand and gave it a gentle squeeze but released it as he steered his truck down the rocky lane to his parents' home. After parking, he turned to her. "Would you like to come in?"

She shook her head. She was tired too. She kept thinking about the letter her father had received today, fearful he might be so swayed that he would suggest letting the boy off the hook. She just couldn't let that happen.

Chase dressed in record time and soon strode out of the house wearing comfortable sweats and a T-shirt. He climbed into the car, turning to her just as he put the key into the ignition. "What's up, Melody? You look worried."

"Just thinking," she murmured, turning to meet his concerned gaze.

"Anything I can do?" he offered helpfully.

She told him about the phone call from the attorney representing the boy who had struck her father. She told him about the letter and also related its details to him. He listened quietly but didn't speak.

"What do you think?" Melody asked finally.

Chase grimaced, unsure if he wanted to talk about anything so heavy right now. Besides, he sensed it was a topic the two might differ on. Chase dealt with kids daily. A twenty-one-year-old in college was still a kid in his book, still dealing with many of the same issues that plagued his students. And the fact was, kids made mistakes. It's what they did—practically part of the job description.

Admittedly, this boy had made a whopper of a mistake, and since Chase adored Tank, it broke his heart to see his friend suffering due to the kid's poor judgment, but things like that happened all the time.

"Can we talk about this later?" Chase asked. "I'm starving and not exactly thinking straight."

And I'm not up for a fight right now, he thought, but he didn't say the words.

Chase and Melody had spent a quiet evening alone together at her place after having shared a pizza and orange soda. They had slipped a DVD into the player and watched a movie Melody hadn't had a chance to see at the theater.

She hadn't realized just how tired she was until, at

one point, she had awakened to find herself in the crook of Chase's arm, with him grinning down at her. He had left soon after.

As Melody drove to the station the next morning, she found Sergeant Moore exiting his patrol car. He waved and motioned her over.

"How are you?" she asked, smiling.

"Good. Hey, I need to talk to you about something. You have a minute?"

"Sure."

Melody followed him into his office and took a seat across from his desk. She watched him expectantly.

"I wanted to tell you a couple of things. I know Manchester mentioned to you that we'll be installing a full-time officer on-site at the school soon. We'll be meeting with Chase Carter to finalize the details tomorrow."

Melody nodded, impressed by how quickly things were moving on that front.

"Also," Moore said, "I wanted to talk to you about another new position opening up in the department."

Melody raised her eyebrows. She hadn't heard about any other opportunities within the department. In fact, she was chomping at the bit to put in for a detective's position, but the positions were still filled and looked as if they might be for some time.

"What's the job, Sarge?" she asked with interest.

"We're looking at establishing a DUI and Traffic Safety Task Force within the department. The aim is to have an officer serve as the coordinator, but this officer would have to work alongside other officers, community members, and offenders. As you well know, driving under the influence has become a huge problem for this department. Something needs to change, and soon."

"What's the objective of this task force?" Melody asked, though she doubted she would be interested in the job. It didn't sound especially exciting, and she knew it wasn't in her to remain behind a desk, fielding phone calls. She needed constant activity to keep her engaged and challenged.

"Well, we're hoping to do quite a lot of community education relating to alcohol abuse. With the college nearby, and all the drinking going on there during the weekends—and during the weekdays," he added with chagrin, "we need to do something to shed some light on the problem. I understand that Chase Carter has actually confiscated open containers of alcohol from kids at the high school. This is getting ridiculous and, as you well know, dangerous."

While she agreed that the community was in dire need of alcohol education, she wasn't necessarily the person to lead the charge. She liked her job too much to give it up for an unknown quantity at this point, though she had been considering her other options quite a lot of late. But she suspected the job of DUI and Traffic Safety Task Force Coordinator would involve a good deal more desk time than road time. No, it wasn't for her.

"Well, I hope this idea pans out," she said. "It sounds like a good one, but . . ."

"You're not interested in heading it up?" Before she could answer, he raised a hand. "Hey, I just wanted to give you a heads-up—give you the chance to mull it over. This isn't going to happen for a while, so think about it."

Melody agreed to do just that and then left him to do his job. She quickly filed a report she'd left from the day before and then headed out to the road, putting herself into service.

She didn't have time to give a thought to the job of DUI and Traffic Safety Task Force Coordinator, since her job required absolute focus. She took one call after the other, wondering how, in such a small town, the citizenry could keep her and her fellow officers so busy.

Chapter Fifteen

"I called Manchester about setting up a meeting between me and the kid who hit me," Tank said matter-of-factly over breakfast.

It was Saturday, and Melody glanced up, meeting his gaze. "You sure that's a good idea, Pop?"

He shrugged. "I guess I won't know for sure until the meeting's over," he admitted. "I don't know. There was something about that letter. He sounded like a good kid. . . ."

Melody huffed as she took her bowl to the sink, dropping it in with a splash. "Well, I wish you wouldn't."

"Melody, when did you get so jaded?" Tank asked, watching her sadly. "Honey, people make mistakes all the time."

"Yeah, well, those mistakes don't usually involve crippling my father." The instant she said the word *crippling,* she regretted it. "Pop, I didn't mean . . ."

"I know," he assured her. "I know."

Melody crossed the room and wrapped an arm around his shoulders. "I love you, you know."

He reached up to pat the side of her face. "I know you do."

Melody heard the crunch of gravel outside. She glanced out the kitchen window and saw Lucy parking her car. "I'm not the only one around here who loves you," Melody grumbled.

Tank arched his eyebrows. "What?"

"Lucy's coming weekends too, now?" she said, incredulous.

Melody was sure she wasn't imagining the hint of color staining her father's cheeks.

"We thought we'd watch a little TV together," he said. "You're leaving, right?"

Melody threw her hands into the air. "You know, I'm going to get a complex if you continue making me feel unwelcome in my own home."

"You know I love you, and you know you're always welcome in *my* home," he corrected with an impish grin.

"I'm definitely leaving now," Melody called with mock indignation as she hurried out of the kitchen and out to the back porch to grab a pair of rain boots. Chase had invited her out to his property today, but she had declined, citing the need to care for her father. But, with Lucy visiting, there was no need for her to stay.

"See you, Pop! Lucy!" she called out.

"Bye," they replied in unison.

Melody was soon in her economy car and heading toward Chase's property. She pulled down the heavily rutted lane and finally managed to pull up beside Chase's truck.

Chase, who was talking to a man Melody didn't recognize from a distance, glanced up. He smiled broadly, motioned to the man to give him a moment, and strode to her car. "Hey, Melody, this is a surprise."

"Lucy's minding Pop," she informed him. "So I got out while the getting was good."

"You should have called me," he said, eyeing her muddied car. "I would have been glad to pick you up in my truck." Chase took her hand and led her to the man. Older, with graying hair, he looked familiar to Melody.

"Melody, this is Dirk Tate. He's the architect helping me finalize design plans on the house."

Melody shook his hand, realizing she had seen him before. She remembered he'd helped a family friend design her home. "Oh, yes, we've actually met before. Good to see you," she told him.

"You too." He turned to Chase. "Well, I'll get busy making the changes we talked about, and I'll call you early next week."

"Sounds good," Chase said.

They watched the man drive off, and Chase draped an arm over her shoulders. Together they walked to the house site, which Melody was surprised to see boasted more than a foundation now. The framing was progressing nicely, and Melody gasped. "Wow! It's coming along, Chase," she enthused.

He nodded. "It is. It should go fairly quickly from here on out." He grinned suddenly, arching his eyebrows suggestively. "Care to step into the master suite?"

She shook her head ruefully and then followed him into the room. He pointed out its special features, which Melody could easily visualize. "Over there will be the tub," he said, "and picture this. Above the tub will be a nearly floor-to-ceiling window framing the mountain view."

He watched her for her response, happy when she broke into a grin.

"That's terrific," she said.

He pointed out features of the master bathroom, including a shower with too many features to mention, he said, as well as double vanities. "Don't want to have to fight you for the sink," he said with a rueful smile.

Melody shot a wide-eyed glance his way. "What did you say, Chase?"

He moved closer to her, taking her hand and staring deeply into her eyes. "I'm sure hoping we're headed in that direction," he said, smiling.

"Are you asking me to marry you?" she asked in alarm, her mouth dropping open.

"No. Not here. Not now. When I propose, I plan to do it right." He chuckled and then leaned toward her, kissing her gently. When they parted, she watched him in awe, warmth traveling from the top of her head to the tips of her toes.

"You took my breath away," Melody commented with a laugh.

"I aim to please. Are you hungry?"

"I had a bowl of cereal a while ago," she told him.

"Well, that's not much. Join me for a bite to eat," he suggested, watching her with an expectant smile.

She followed him to his truck, where he pulled out a picnic basket. Hand in hand they walked back to the house and into the future kitchen. Chase pulled up a plastic chair and then dashed to a different room to grab another one. He made a makeshift table by placing a flat board atop a tall bucket.

When he pulled out a cloth and spread it over the table and then laid out the food he'd packed, Melody gasped. He pulled out croissants, strawberries dipped in chocolate, and an assortment of cheeses. Sparkling cider rounded out the delectable spread.

"Chase Carter, how did you know I'd be here?" Melody asked.

"How do you know I packed this for you?" he teased.

"Now you're skating on thin ice, buddy," she threatened.

He raised his hands as if in surrender. "You know this is for you. Everything I do is for you."

"Ah, you're so sweet," she quipped. "Tell me. How'd you know?"

"I have special powers," he said crisply, his eyes alight with humor.

"Do tell," she said, narrowing her eyes. "I mean, *do* tell."

"Oh, all right," he grumbled. "I heard Aunt Lucy say she was heading to your house, so I figured it wouldn't be long before Tank tossed you out on your ear."

She hid her smile, endeavoring to sound miffed. "My dad would never toss me out on my ear," she protested.

"On your butt, then?" Chase quipped.

She gasped, and he reached out and took her hand. "What matters is, you're here."

The twosome ate, thoroughly enjoying each other's company. Melody realized that Chase was demonstrating his feelings for her daily. Aside from the flowers and candy, he often called her to leave sweet messages on her voice mail. He sometimes called her at the end of the workday to ask how her shift had gone, and he even sent her silly or sentimental cards conveying his love.

Melody smiled at him now, a wide smile that transformed her face and conveyed her happiness, and he grinned back. He reached across the tiny tabletop, threading his fingers into her hair as he cupped the back of her head. He drew her close. She anticipated the kiss, filling with pleasure when their lips met.

When he pulled back, he gave a sigh of contentment.

"I could do that all day long," he said, smiling like the cat that had swallowed a canary.

"I don't know about all day . . ." Melody said as she stood and rounded the tiny table. She stared into his eyes, seeing the love there, and dropped her head and kissed *him* this time. She pressed with a gentle insistence, and he surprised her by pulling her onto his lap. She chuckled, her lips still hovering over his and tingling with the fire of their attraction.

She kissed him again, and when she finally ended the kiss, he slumped weakly against the back of the chair. He ran a hand through his hair, meeting her gaze. His voice was husky when he spoke. "Wow! Shall we try that again?"

Melody surprised him when she slipped from his grasp before he had time to register what was happening. She took a step back, grinning at him. "We'd better stop now," she quipped. "We're not married yet, you know."

"Good point," Chase acknowledged, standing up and dropping his gaze to her lovely face.

When Melody's cell phone suddenly trilled in her hand, she practically leaped out of her skin. She raised an index finger, gesturing for him to give her a minute.

She answered the phone, surprised to hear Lucy's frantic voice at the other end of the line.

"Oh, Melody, your father has fallen again, and I can't manage to get him up." She said the words in a rush, and Melody attempted to make sense of them.

"Lucy, did you say Pop fell again?"

"Yes. Please, Melody, come quickly. And bring Chase. Tank hit his head on the edge of the kitchen counter, and I think he may need stitches."

"I'll be right there," Melody said, and she hung up. She turned to Chase. "Pop fell."

"Let's go." He took hold of Melody's hand, and together they ran to his truck.

They hurriedly climbed in, and Chase turned the vehicle around so he could drive out nose first. He sped toward the road, fishtailing before he left the mud behind and hit the concrete roadway.

They arrived at Melody's home in record time, each jumping down from the truck simultaneously and charging into the house. They found Lucy kneeling on the floor, pressing a towel to the back of Tank's head.

"Oh, thank God you're both here," Lucy cried. "I wanted to call for an ambulance, but Tank wouldn't let me. I just know he needs stitches."

Melody gingerly stepped over her father's legs, forcing back her fear. She took a deep, steading breath, praying her emergency training would prevail and she could manage to keep a cool head. She took the towel away from her father's head and winced. The gash was deep and spewing blood.

Chase knelt down behind her. "Melody, head injuries always bleed a lot. It's just the way it is," he murmured soothingly into her ear. Chase leaned around her and grasped Tank's shoulder, giving him an encouraging squeeze. "Tank, you're going to be just fine. But we do need to call for an ambulance."

Tank objected loudly. "I don't need an ambulance."

"We'd rather be safe than sorry," Chase said firmly. "You could have a concussion, or worse. It's an ambulance for you, buddy."

Chase stood up and turned to Melody. "Honey, call 911."

A police officer arrived at the house within moments, followed by a screaming ambulance.

Chase helped Melody up, and she was glad for his hand. She felt slightly dizzy from the sight of her father's blood on the kitchen floor. Together they moved aside to allow the emergency medical technician to work on Tank.

Melody noticed that Lucy appeared wobbly as she tried to stand, and she rushed to the woman's side, grasping her arm. "Are you all right?" she asked with concern, noting that the woman looked to be near tears.

"I'll be all right when I know Tank is all right," she said tremulously, and then she burst into tears.

"We all will," Melody said, wrapping the distraught woman in an embrace.

As Tank was loaded into the ambulance, Chase and Melody helped Lucy into Chase's truck. Fortunately, the tall truck had running boards, so the woman was able to step up fairly easily. Melody had already grown used to the raised cab, so she swung into it without a problem.

At the hospital, doctors ran several tests on Tank but determined he had suffered no more than a bad cut and a slight concussion. They did, however, determine that his blood pressure was higher than normal and opted to keep him in the hospital overnight for observation.

He'd grumbled, of course, but with his broken leg, it wasn't as if he could make an escape, though he did threaten.

Melody, Chase, and Lucy remained by his bed for several hours until the hospital staff finally shooed them out.

Lucy first stepped to his bedside, watching him with a concerned expression. "I'll be here first thing in the morning," she told him, and then she kissed him lovingly on the cheek. Melody moved to his other side and kissed him on the other cheek. Chase shook his hand.

With a final good-bye, they headed for the door, only to step aside when Ed and Mary suddenly burst into the room, out of breath and wearing concerned expressions on their faces.

"Tank, are you okay, buddy?" Ed asked. "We just got Chase's message."

"I'm okay," Tank assured his friends.

"You had us worried, Tank," Mary said.

Ed moved to stand beside Tank's bed. "What'd you do this time?"

"Same old," Tank said simply. "But with a new twist. I conked my head."

A nurse suddenly entered the room and announced that the earlier visitors needed to leave—*now*—while the newcomers could stay a few short minutes.

The threesome left Tank's room, promising to return in the morning. Chase took Melody's hand and draped his other arm over his aunt's shoulders. "Don't you worry, Aunt Lucy," he said. "It'll take something mightier than a kitchen counter to keep ol' Tank down."

Lucy nodded numbly, and Melody studied her anguished face. It was as clear to Melody as the tears on Lucy's face—Lucy loved Tank.

Chapter Sixteen

Later that night, Melody called her father's hospital room to check on him. He answered with a groggy hello.

"How're you feeling, Pop?"

"Oh, good. A little tired. I'm missing my own bed. These hospital contraptions definitely weren't built for slumber."

"I know, but you'll be home and in your own bed tomorrow."

"Hey, honey, don't forget to lock up the house tonight. It worries me, your being there all alone."

"Pop, I'm fine," she said crisply. "Besides, I'm not alone right now," she told him. "Chase is with me. You stop worrying, and try to get a good night's rest."

"I'll try. Love you, Mel."

"You too."

Melody replaced the phone on the hook and smiled at Chase.

"How is he?" Chase asked.

"He sounded tired but okay. He's worried about me."

"He is? Obviously he hasn't seen you drop a guy three times your size."

"It's a trick I only pull out of my bag when I really want to impress somebody."

"Oh," Chase said with a smile. "You know, you don't have to impress me. You can kiss me, however."

"Be glad to," Melody said with a laugh. She sat down beside him and turned to him, her lips parted slightly and enticingly.

Chase claimed her lips. When Melody finally pulled back, she gave a sigh of pleasure. "That was nice," she told him.

Chase smiled and watched her thoughtfully before glancing around the room. Suddenly the four walls around them appeared to hold his rapt attention. She watched him, curious.

"I was just thinking, I'll be glad to get my house finished," Chase told her then. "It's coming along."

"Your folks will miss you," Melody pointed out, eyeing him.

"I'll be right up the road," he said. "Hey, any news about my stolen goods?" he inquired suddenly. "I was really hoping they might turn up, since I'll have to replace the copper wire soon, and it's expensive," he added ruefully.

Melody wondered, how had they gone from kissing to talk of work so swiftly? "So much for our romantic moment," Melody muttered as she straightened on the couch. "Uh, no, we haven't turned up anything on your stolen goods. You'll be the first to know when we do."

"Have other people reported break-ins lately?" Chase asked with interest.

Melody shot him a hostile glance.

Chase chuckled. "Okay, enough shop talk. You wanna watch some TV?" he asked.

Melody pinned him with a gaze. "So much for our *romantic* moment," she repeated in measured tones, emphasizing *romantic*. Apparently her words hadn't registered the first time.

Chase grinned. "You know, I realized I should try to be on my best behavior, since, well, your giant father isn't here to chaperone, but you're not making it easy for me. See what a good guy I am? I'm thinking I'd probably make somebody a pretty fine husband someday," Chase said, reaching for her hand.

Melody chuckled. "Kiss me now. We'll worry about the someday later."

Chase smoothed a hand through her hair, staring into her eyes. "You have beautiful eyes," he commented.

"Yeah, yeah, beautiful," Melody grumbled.

"Nice lips too," Chase added with a laugh.

"Now you're talking," Melody said, leaning toward him and kissing him soundly on the lips. He wrapped her in a hug, and she heard a sigh of contentment escape his lips.

Suddenly, the phone rang, and Melody grumbled. She rose slowly and picked it up on the third ring. "Hello."

"Hello, Mel," Ed said. "Is that son of mine anywhere close?"

"Not close enough," Melody muttered to herself, but she passed Chase the phone.

She watched his face, noting how the corners of his lips twitched into a smile. "I know, Dad. No. I won't stay long. Yep. I understand that Melody needs her rest. Yep. Yep. No, wouldn't want to do that. Me too."

Chase leaned forward to hang up the phone, biting back his laughter until the phone was securely on the hook. He threw his head back and laughed heartily. "Dad just lectured me on how to treat a lady. Good grief. Does he not know I'm the poster boy for gentlemanly behavior? I mean, have I not shown the utmost restraint this very evening?"

Melody dropped onto the couch beside him again. "Gentlemanly, huh? TV?" she asked with a disgruntled laugh.

They sat in companionable silence, Melody resting her head on Chase's shoulder as they watched a comedy on television. She began falling asleep, but when Chase gently slipped off the couch and stood, she woke with a start, glancing around.

"I should go," Chase told her softly. "You need your rest."

She nodded and stood.

"Aunt Lucy and I will pick you up in the morning, then—say, ten-thirty?"

She nodded again and yawned.

He smiled into her eyes. "Do you need help with anything around here before I go? Did you remember to lock the back door?"

"I'll get it," she told him. "No worries."

"If you need me, call, okay?"

Melody hid her smile. Chase was being so chivalrous. "Will do," she assured him.

"Okay, then," he said, and he kissed her gently on the lips.

Melody followed him to the door, and he brushed a kiss across her cheek before striding out to his truck. She closed the door behind him, smiling as she walked through the house, checking to be sure all the doors were locked.

Finally she went to bed, only to awaken a couple of hours later to the sound of breaking glass. She sat up rapidly, blinking her eyes and listening intently. The sound had been close but distant enough not to have been in the main house. She rose from the bed, deciding the sound must have come from the storage shed out back.

Melody padded across her bedroom, opting to keep the light off as she searched for her robe. She slipped into it and her pink slippers and then retrieved her .45 from her bedside table. Since she was home alone, she hadn't locked it away in her gun safe as she normally did. She quickly took the safety off and carefully positioned her finger near the trigger.

She tiptoed along the hallway and then down the stairs to the main level of the house. She crossed the kitchen to the back door but paused for a moment to scan the backyard. Her eyes lighted on the shed, and she squinted against the darkness. Was someone out there? she wondered, and she strained to see if a window had been broken.

It was no use; she couldn't tell. But suddenly she spied a lone figure round the shed and then disappear behind it. She padded back to the antiquated phone in the kitchen. She dialed 911 and advised dispatch to send a car. "The shed's out back, behind the main house. No sirens," she directed. "I don't want 'em to know you're coming."

She hurried to the back door and quietly pulled it open. She stepped outside but dropped low to the ground when she spied one intruder, and then another, moving around the perimeter of the shed. They spoke in hushed whispers, and she realized one figure carried something large, since she could see the silhouette of the item in his arms.

Melody held the pistol in outstretched arms, aiming

it squarely in front of her as she stealthily crossed the lawn, careful to duck for cover behind trees or shrubs when possible. She had nearly reached the shed when one of the intruders spotted her.

"Hey!" he shouted. "Who's there?"

Melody aimed the pistol at the man, who took a step or two closer to her. He squinted as he tried to see her clearly.

"Police. Get down on the ground," she told him, and to his friend, she said, "You, too."

She heard the closer of the two speak. "Yeah, right," he said with a sardonic chuckle.

"I'm a police officer, and I'm telling you one more time. Get down on the ground."

Suddenly she heard the man behind him. "She is a cop. You'd better do what she says."

The nearer of the two continued to laugh, but his friend dropped onto his stomach, raising his hands to his head.

"Get down on the ground," Melody said firmly to the other man, who failed to comply.

In the darkness under a canopy of trees, Melody could barely discern the man's features. She sensed that the guy on the ground was young, maybe a teenager, but this guy . . . It was hard to tell.

He was of medium height but muscular, and she assessed his posture, wondering if his resistance was a show of bravado or the real thing.

Suddenly the guy took a quick step toward her, and

Melody's finger curled toward the trigger. "Don't do it," she warned. "I'll drop you so fast, the devil won't have time to put out a welcome mat."

He chuckled menacingly, and Melody stiffened, ready . . .

Suddenly several officers rounded the main house, their flashlights illuminating the yard.

"You all right, Mel?" She recognized Andy Benton's voice, and then his face came into view, along with those of several other officers.

Andy aimed his revolver at the intruder, who promptly dropped to the ground.

Melody felt relief wash over her. She hadn't wanted to shoot the guy, but she would have. Had he taken one more step toward her . . .

"Never a dull moment, eh, Mel?" Andy commented.

"No kidding," she said. "I didn't think he was going to comply. Probably wouldn't have if you guys hadn't showed up. If he'd taken one more step, I was going to drop him," she said loudly for the guy's benefit.

Soon officers cuffed the suspects and hauled them to their feet. They were taken to patrol cars, while Andy took the report from Melody. "I'll write up a supplemental sometime tomorrow," she told him. "I have to go by the hospital in the morning to pick up my dad, but I can probably have it done by late tomorrow afternoon."

Melody followed the officers to the front of the house, and it wasn't until the motion-sensor lights popped on that she remembered how she was dressed. Her robe wasn't so bad, but the baby doll nightie beneath and the pink slippers on her feet . . .

When her fellow officers chuckled, she refused to give them the satisfaction of responding. No doubt word of her sleep attire would work its way around the station's rumor mill. *Great, just great.*

Melody turned when she heard the crunch of gravel as another vehicle drove up. She saw it was a truck and realized it was Chase.

He was out of the truck in a heartbeat, running to Melody's side and clutching her shoulders. "Are you all right? We saw the flashing lights from the house."

She smiled. "Fine. You?"

He shook his head ruefully, and then his eyes traveled the length of her body. He took in the shortie robe and pink slippers. And the nightie beneath . . . "What happened, Melody?" he asked, attempting to focus.

"Oh, I had a break-in. Couple of guys broke out a window in the shed out back and started hauling stuff out."

Chase noticed that as she spoke, she gestured with the gun at the end of her arm as if it were an extension of her hand. She saw him watching her and chuckled. "Don't worry. The safety is on."

"It's not that," he muttered. "It's just . . ."

"What?"

"Nothing." He wasn't about to tell her that the sight of her in her sleepwear and pink slippers and wielding a gun simply seemed . . . surreal. Nor was he about to tell her that the thought of her warding off intruders all alone terrified him.

An officer approached them. "Well, Mel," the man said, "we'll take 'em downtown and process 'em. They'll be lodged in the jail."

She nodded. "Ten to one, if we check out their garages, we'll find there isn't room for a car in either one." Suddenly her eyes widened. "Chase, I'll bet we've solved the mystery of your missing items too."

"I hope so," he said. Chase draped an arm around her as the officers pulled down the drive and headed back to the station.

Melody sighed with satisfaction.

"What was that for?" Chase asked.

"Another good night's work," she said, nodding crisply.

Chase refrained from asking for details. He feared if he did, first she'd tell him something that was liable to shake him up, and second, he didn't want her thinking he was questioning her ability to handle herself in a hairy situation. Ignorance was bliss, and . . . Melody was amazing.

"Brrr, I'm cold," she said, rubbing her arms briskly. "I had so much adrenaline surging through my body, I didn't even register the chill before," she marveled.

"Let's get inside," Chase suggested, looking around furtively as if he expected a third intruder to pop out from behind a tree.

Inside the house, Chase followed Melody to the living room, where she sat down on the couch. She propped her feet on the coffee table and studied her slippers, which were coated with mud. "Darn," she muttered. "Ruined my slippers."

Chase dropped onto the couch beside her. "I'll get you another pair."

"Really?"

"Sure."

Melody smiled and then yawned. "You should go home and get some sleep," she told him, resting her head on his shoulder.

"I should," he said, but he made no move to go. However, when Melody fell asleep beside him, he rose to leave. He found himself wanting to stay, to keep an eye on her as she slept. The burglary had him more riled than he cared to admit, but he knew it was best that he not stay. If he did, his parents would likely give him a tongue-lashing to rival anything he'd earned when he was a mischievous lad. His dad had already given him a speech about protecting his lady love's virtue, and he was well aware that tongues did wag in small towns.

Chase urged Melody to lie down. He draped a throw over her, kissed her cheek, and then silently padded out of the house. He checked the front door to be sure it was locked and strode silently to his truck.

Chapter Seventeen

Chase and his aunt picked up Melody the next morning. The group drove to the hospital, eager to check on Tank.

When they arrived, they found he already had a visitor. Melody didn't recognize the young man standing at her father's bedside.

She shot her father a questioning gaze. "Melody, I'd like you to meet Justin Morgan."

Melody gasped, and Chase turned to her stricken face. He moved to stand beside her, draping a protective arm over her shoulders. Melody appreciated his support, since she wasn't sure how she felt about coming face-to-face with the boy who had driven drunk and seriously injured her father.

208

The young man met her gaze and then extended a trembling hand to her. Melody hesitated briefly before clasping his hand. Chase shook the boy's hand next, and then Lucy greeted him.

Melody shook her head, perplexed. "How'd you know my dad was in the hospital?" she asked the young man. She still wasn't certain how she felt about his being there.

"I made the papers," Tank volunteered with a self-deprecating laugh. "I imagine the headline read, 'Moronic police commander conks own head.'"

The boy glanced at Tank, his lips twitching into a smile—almost.

"Justin here came to apologize to me for the accident. He wanted to contact me before, but his attorney told him it wouldn't be prudent to speak to me."

"And why is it suddenly prudent for Justin to speak to you?" Melody demanded, suspicious. "Perhaps because the prosecutors have completed their investigation, and it appears that Justin will be charged for his crime?"

Justin straightened, meeting Melody's angry eyes dead on. "I'm prepared to suffer the consequences of my actions," he said firmly. "I did a horrible thing, and I deserve to pay."

"You know you may do jail time," Melody told him, her eyes narrowed angrily.

"I understand that," he said. "But I also believe I

should have met Mr. Hudson face-to-face a long time ago. I should have gone to the hospital to check on him. I should have . . ." He raked a hand through his hair and nearly broke down. He took a deep, steadying breath. "He deserved an apology. And it's about time he got it."

With that, the boy nodded at Tank and then strode out of the room. To Melody's surprise, Chase followed him.

Melody suddenly felt bereft, as if she might crumble and fall to the floor and into a million pieces without Chase there to hold her up. Seeing the boy who had injured her father had taken a toll. The kid's stupidity could very well have cost her father his life that day. Lucy apparently noticed that Melody was in a tenuous state and moved to stand beside her, draping a supportive arm around her back.

Melody offered her a tremulous smile and to everyone's surprise, including her own, burst into tears. Lucy wrapped her in a hug, and that's how Chase found her when he stepped back into the room.

"What's this?" he asked, moving to extract Melody from Lucy's arms and cocking his head to look into her face. Tears continued to pool in her blue eyes, spilling over onto her cheeks. Chase smiled into her eyes. "Let's talk, okay?"

He took her hand and led her out of the room. He guided her to an outdoor sitting area, and the two sat down on a bench. Melody sniffled and swiped at her eyes. Chase watched her sympathetically.

"Tell me what's on your mind, Melody," he said softly.

She sniffled again. "I've been hating that boy since the day of the accident, and it turns out he's not a bad kid at all," she blubbered. "He feels awful for what he's done."

"I know. I spoke to him. He seems very sincere to me and is more than ready to face the music."

"I feel terrible," she moaned.

"Well, don't. You're only human."

Later, back at home and with Tank settled comfortably in his bed, Melody sat at his bedside, watching him with concern. "How do you feel, Pop?"

"Stupid," he muttered. "Very stupid."

"Anybody could have fallen in their kitchen and hit their head on the sharp edge of a countertop," she said, and then she grinned. "Well, some people anyway."

"I'm tall," he said, as if that explained it. "I'm always bumping my head into something."

"It's like me," Melody said. "I'm short, so I'm usually the one taking an elbow in the nose or eye when I'm in a crowd."

The two commiserated for a moment, but then the talk turned serious.

"Melody, I'm going to talk to the prosecutor's office. I don't want to see that boy charged. It'll ruin his life."

"He has to face some consequences of his actions," Melody pointed out.

"I know," Tank said. "You know, late last night, Manchester showed up at the hospital to visit. He mentioned they're thinking about establishing a DUI and Traffic Safety Task Force at the department. He mentioned that they had you in mind to serve as coordinator. . . ."

"Not interested," Melody cut in. "I'd be bored to tears."

"Honey, this town needs something like that. With all these kids getting into cars and driving drunk, along with all the irresponsible adults doing the same thing, we really need to get into the schools and start educating these kids."

"I agree," Melody said, "but I'm not sure I'm the one to head the task force. You know me, I like to be on the go." She paused, and Tank watched her. "I haven't told you, Pop, but I *have* been thinking it might be time for me to get off the road for a while. I've been there nearly five years, and I'm considering going into a specialized unit if an opening comes up."

"What would you like to do?"

"Well, truth be told, I'd like to go into the detectives' unit, but, as you know, it's full and will be for some time."

"Anything else interest you?" Tank asked.

"I don't know, maybe traffic enforcement or even truck enforcement. My hours would be set, which would free me up to join the SWAT team."

Tank stifled a groan. That was his worst fear—his

daughter on the SWAT team. She'd probably end up in charge. Lord knew, she was a crack shot.

"So you've definitely ruled out the task force?" Tank asked.

"I haven't actually ruled out anything."

"Well, regardless of who oversees it, I was thinking there might be a way to get Justin Morgan involved," Tank said. "He mentioned to me that he forces himself everyday to look at a photo from the newspaper of the EMTs taking me away in an ambulance as a reminder of what he did and what could happen if he ever drinks to excess again. I was thinking maybe I could suggest as part of his sentencing that he give talks to kids about the dangers of driving while intoxicated."

Melody nodded. "It sounds like a good idea. Maybe we could shock some sense into kids if they see what can happen to them or someone else if they drive while under the influence."

"I'll give Manchester a call," Tank said, and then he eyed her speculatively. "You really wouldn't be interested in acting as coordinator of a task force?" he asked. "It's actually a compliment to be considered, you know. They obviously believe you're the one with the skills to get the job done, or they wouldn't have suggested you. You know, Mel, it's unusual for the department to even approach someone prior to an official posting of a job opening."

Melody noted that Tank looked awfully proud of

her, and she smiled. "I'm going to leave you to rest, Pop. Lucy mentioned she'll be coming over in a couple of hours. She said she's bringing you dinner."

Tank smiled fondly, and Melody heard a contented sigh escape his lips. "Pop, are you in love?" she asked.

"I . . . uh . . . well . . ." he stammered.

"I'll take that as a yes," Melody said, and then she left him so he could rest.

Melody wanted to tackle some light housekeeping but found that Lucy had the place spiffy and clean. She went outside to see if anything needed her attention.

She first checked on the rosebush Chase had brought her, noting with pleasure that it seemed to be doing just fine. From there, she headed to the barn and found a rake and a leaf blower. There was so much debris accumulating on the walkways around the house, she needed to do some clearing.

Melody attacked the debris with a vengeance, piling dirt and fallen leaves into a tidy pile. She dashed to the back porch and found a huge plastic garbage bag and then dashed back outside. To her surprise and pleasure, she found Chase standing over the pile, looking for all intents and purposes as if he intended to jump in.

"Don't you dare, Chase Carter," she warned. "I've been working for hours."

"Well, since you used my last name . . ." he said in mock terror.

He stepped around the pile and took her into his

arms. "You smell like spring," he said, pressing his nose to the top of her head.

She chuckled. "What does spring smell like? And you'd better not say sweaty."

"Nope." He sniffed again. "Actually, you smell more like citrus."

Melody gasped. "You must have the most sensitive nose on the planet. My shampoo is citrus."

He chuckled. "No, I saw the shampoo in your bathroom."

"You're a fraud!" she exclaimed. "And I'm . . . tired."

"Are you up for dinner?" he asked.

"Well, Lucy is coming over soon, and I imagine she and Pop would enjoy some quiet time. Right now, he's on his back in his bed and, hopefully, resting."

" 'Hopefully,' " Chase said with a wince. "Here's hoping he doesn't fall out of bed."

"Oh, he did that before," Melody told him.

Chase chuckled. "Really?"

"Yeah, the leg went, and the rest of him followed."

"Oh, poor Tank." Chase laughed. "Well, we definitely won't leave until Lucy gets here, and then we'll prop pillows around him to prevent him from taking another tumble."

"I'm going to run inside and take a shower," Melody told him. "Will you wait in the kitchen for me?"

"Absolutely."

She hurried into the house and upstairs to her room, showering and readying herself in no time. She dressed in jeans and a soft blue sweater. The color brought out the blue of her eyes. When she entered the kitchen, Chase whistled approvingly.

She noticed he'd shed his jacket, and she nearly whistled at him. He wore a short-sleeved shirt, and the constricting bands of fabric on his biceps emphasized his muscular arms. She stared at them, and he noticed. He opened his arms to her, and she stepped into them.

"I could hang out here all day," she murmured.

When somebody cleared her throat behind them, Melody spun around. She grinned at Lucy, who came in laden with food.

"For me?" Chase teased.

"I'm sure Tank will share," Lucy said with a laugh. "Would you mind getting the rest of the food out of my trunk, Chase?"

Melody stepped away from Chase, and he rose obligingly. "Will do, Auntie."

Chase headed outside, and Lucy shot him an affectionate glance, then turned to Melody. "How's your dad, honey?"

"He's resting now but looking forward to your visit."

Lucy smiled and sought Melody's eyes. "Honey, I want to thank you for . . ."

"What?" Melody asked, curious.

"Well, for showing me kindness. I know your mother passed only three years ago, and I understand you two were very close. I also understand it must be difficult for you that your father and I are growing fond of each other."

"I think . . . you're good for Pop," Melody admitted, realizing it was true. Her father had been in a funk—a depression, really—since her mother passed, and now his outlook seemed much more positive, even in light of his injury.

"Thank you, Melody. I appreciate your saying so. And I hope we two can be good friends."

"I'm sure we will," Melody said, but she turned when Chase stepped into the kitchen, arms laden with containers.

"There's enough here to feed an army," he said. "Even Tank can't possibly eat it all."

"Most of those go into the freezer," Lucy told him, eyeing him ruefully.

"I guess it's true what they say: the way to a man's heart is through his stomach," Chase quipped.

Lucy's eyes widened in shock, and then she whacked Chase on the shoulder. "You stop that."

"Hey, sorry, sorry. Didn't mean to upset you."

"Weren't you leaving?" Lucy asked him, eyes sparkling merrily.

Chapter Eighteen

Melody hated to leave her father Monday morning, but she knew he was in Lucy's capable hands. The woman had fussed over him all weekend, and Tank seemed to enjoy the attention.

When Melody arrived at work, first thing she found a message from Commander Manchester. He wanted to see her.

She stopped by his office to see if he happened to be there. He wasn't, and she wasn't able to try again until late afternoon. Finally back at the station after a long day of calls, she knocked lightly on his door. He called for her to enter, smiling as she stepped into his office.

"Hey, I just spoke to your dad. He mentioned that the boy who plowed into him stopped by his hospital room the other day."

Melody nodded. "He apologized for the accident."

"I know. Your dad seems insistent he doesn't want him charged but suggested he participate in some type of alcohol-education program. He mentioned something about the kid speaking at local schools about the dangers of alcohol abuse."

Melody nodded. "Pop's afraid if the kid does jail time, it'll destroy his future."

"Your dad is mighty softhearted," Manchester said. "But I do trust his judgment. I'll see what I can do to start the wheels turning."

"Is that why you wanted to see me?" Melody asked, but then she realized she had received a message from him before he'd actually spoken to her father.

"No, actually, I wanted to talk to you a little more about the task force coordinator's position. Melody, you do understand that this is a promotion, being that it's a specialized position, and that you'd realize a substantial pay increase?"

Melody's eyes widened. No. She hadn't realized that. Nobody had told her.

"Does that change anything for you? The truth is, we'd really like to see you in the position. We think you're well-suited to the job. You're a go-getter, and the fact is, you'd be the face of the program. We need someone with your enthusiasm to get the ball rolling."

"I'm . . . flattered," Melody told him, "and I am considering it. But you know how much I like to be where the action is."

He watched her speculatively, opened his mouth to speak, then promptly clamped it shut.

"Was there something else?" Melody asked.

He shook his head. "No. Just this—please give the job some thought. You have a couple of weeks before we put out a department-wide job posting, so you might want to strike while the iron is hot."

"I'll take that under advisement," she said. "And I do want to thank you for everything."

He nodded, and Melody left the room and headed to her patrol car and home. As she drove, her mind kept going back to the conversation with Manchester. The department heads seemed intent on her taking on the job, but she wasn't sure she was the best fit. Oh, well, she had a couple of weeks to mull it over.

As she drove toward home, reviewing the day's events, she suddenly started when a car roared past her, nearly colliding with oncoming traffic when it veered out of its lane. Melody sped up, flipped the switch to activate her emergency lights, and turned on the siren. Next she alerted dispatch she was in pursuit of a vehicle.

She felt a surge of adrenaline as the car surged forward. Cars ahead of her fanned out to the right, allowing her to pass, and she remained on the bumper of the car whose driver seemed unwilling to pull over. Melody carefully reached for the megaphone and instructed the driver to pull the car over. Still the car didn't stop. She called for backup, advising dispatch of her current location.

To her horror, the car sped up even more, and she watched it veer precariously to the right, straddling the fog line and nearly plunging into a shallow ravine. Melody winced but remained in pursuit. She feared that this driver would certainly kill somebody if he or she didn't stop soon.

Finally the car straddled the center line and nearly clipped an eighteen-wheeler in the opposite lane. The driver then veered right to avoid the collision and spun out of control. The car careered off the road, clipped a telephone pole along the passenger side, and finally came to rest in a field.

Melody slowed to a stop and radioed dispatch with the location of the accident. She asked for an ambulance and then hurried to check on the car's driver and occupants. She pulled her pistol, her arm outstretched, her senses alert and at the ready. Unsure what she would find, she cautiously approached the vehicle, holstering her gun when she realized that the car was full of teenagers, and all were slumped in their seats, except one.

Melody winced. A boy of about sixteen had been ejected from the vehicle, his body lying in a crumpled heap near a tree stump. She hurried to his side first, checking for a pulse. It was faint but, thankfully, there.

She quickly checked the other kids—two girls and a

boy—for a pulse, and with relief realized all were alive. She smelled a strong odor of intoxicants emanating from the vehicle, and she grimaced. The kids had clearly been drinking.

To her relief, backup arrived, followed by two ambulances with blaring siren. A fire truck was soon onsite as well, and Melody stepped aside to allow the rescue personnel to do their jobs. When the Traffic Homicide Investigators arrived, she was glad to hand the investigation of the serious-injury accident over to them.

She would, however, be responsible for compiling the initial report, and she began attempting to obtain the information she needed. She cautiously approached as the rescue workers tended to the kids. She did her best to obtain identification from each victim and secured school IDs from the wallets of the two boys. She also found an ID in a purse belonging to one of the girls.

When the teenagers were finally taken off in ambulances, she remained behind, assisting the Traffic Homicide team as best she could and describing in detail what she had observed just before the teenage driver lost control and left the roadway. When everybody finally cleared the scene, Melody turned her patrol car around and headed to the station. Although she had been on her way home and was looking forward to an evening with Chase, her plans had most definitely changed.

At the station, she called Chase at his folks' house

and told him she would be unable to meet him and why.

"They were local kids?" he asked, emitting a haggard sigh.

"Yes."

"Do you recall their names?"

Melody told him.

"I recognize two of the names," he said sadly, and then his voice rose in anguish. "What's going on with these kids, Melody? They're bright. They know they're putting their lives on the line when they drink and drive."

"They're teenagers, Chase. They think they've invincible, and they think alcohol is some sort of magic, happy potion. I don't know, I guess when they drink, they think they're grown-up."

"Something has to give," he said softly. "Well, Mel, try not to work too late, and be careful driving home. I love you, you know."

"I know. I love you too."

By the next day, it seemed the whole community had heard about the wreck the night before, and everyone was talking about it. Melody received countless calls from concerned citizens while she sat at her desk, trying to finish a follow-up report.

She was just filing the report when Manchester approached her desk. "Have you given any more thought to the task force coordinator position?" he asked.

"I haven't really had a chance to," she said evasively. "I've been so busy."

In truth, Melody *had* thought about it, as she lay awake the night before and, in her mind's eye, saw the injured teens as if she were watching a movie that played over and over. The mental picture still made her cringe. While she understood why she was so disturbed by the tragedy, she was usually better able to compartmentalize, to forget, and to move on quickly. It wasn't that she was callous; it was simply a coping mechanism. But now . . .

Manchester nodded crisply. "I thought, well, in light of the accident . . ." He shook his head and smiled sadly. "Well, anyway, think about it."

Melody watched his retreating figure, realizing just how much he wanted her to take the position. She wondered, if she rejected the job offer, would it reflect badly on her? She hadn't considered that possibility before. She knew, in reality, she could be forced to accept the position. She had signed on to protect and serve, and her superiors could wield their authority and force her into the position. She doubted they would do that, however.

When the phone rang at her desk, she snatched it up, smiling when she heard Chase's voice at the end of the line.

"How's it going?" he asked.

"Oh, all right," she said.

"You sound tired."

"I am. I got home late last night," she said.

"Me too. After talking to you, I went by the hospital to check on the kids. I just spoke to the mother of one of them a minute or so ago."

"How are they doing?" Melody asked.

"Three are out of the woods, but David Lange, the boy who was ejected from the car, is in coma. His parents are beyond distraught."

"I can imagine," Melody commiserated.

"I don't know how you do it, Mel," he said suddenly.

"What?"

"See the things you see, day in and day out. I don't think I could do it."

Melody was quiet, processing the statement. She'd heard it before. She wondered, was Chase trying to wield his influence, hoping she might give up her job because he found aspects of it unpalatable?

"Are we still on for dinner tonight?" she said, changing the subject.

He perceived the change in her voice and noted her swift shift in subject matter. "I'm sorry," he murmured.

"Why are you sorry?"

"I can hear in your voice that I upset you."

"You didn't upset me. It's just . . ."

"Tell me."

"You know, Chase, I get that you're not particularly pleased about my line of work. And I'm sorry it's difficult for you, and . . ." She paused, searching for the right words.

"Melody, that's not true. . . ." he said.

"Hear me out. I can't help but wonder if your feelings about my job will eventually cause a rift between us—if it'll prove too much for you to handle. I don't know how I'd deal with it if you find you can't deal with my job."

"Melody, I told you, I can handle it. You seem intent on projecting feelings onto me that I don't actually own. I can't say I'm not going to worry about you when you're working, but I'd never ask you to give up your job. And nothing could keep me from you now that I've found you again. I love you, Mel."

Melody wished she could believe him—believe in him. Why were doubts suddenly pressing on her shoulders like overfilled sandbags?

Melody drove toward home in her patrol car, eager to slip into a warm bath. It was almost eight o'clock, and she felt bone weary. Earlier Chase had asked her to dinner, but because she'd been held up at work again, she had called to cancel. He had said he understood, but she wasn't certain. She had heard a note in his voice that worried her.

Melody really felt fatigued, as if she had the weight of the world on her shoulders still. Sometimes it was like that at night. She'd arrive home eager to wash away every trace of her job—to forget something or someone that had affected her in a way that left her sad, angry, or uncomfortable.

She knew she couldn't save the world, but sometimes she found she couldn't save anyone during the course of a day. People tended to make bad choice after bad choice, and no matter what she said or did, she knew that the next day, they'd go on making those same bad choices. And then she would show up again, maybe a day later, maybe a week later, and continue a cycle that left her mentally weary.

When suddenly dispatch called her on her radio, requesting her location, she wished for once she could ignore the call. It was an interesting revelation. She never avoided calls. Some officers were adept at the art of looking busy so as to force dispatch to foist a call onto the more hardworking officers.

She reached for her radio. "Control One David Two." Melody responded with her call sign.

"What's your location?"

"Heading home."

"Please divert to the Topper Tavern at Junction 13 for a bar fight."

"Copy."

Melody quickly turned around and drove to the tavern approximately three miles away in the opposite direction. She reached the bar just as several other units arrived on the scene. She joined the other officers as they gathered in the parking lot to discuss a plan of action.

"How many are there?" Melody asked.

"Six, according to a caller who dialed 911," someone volunteered.

"All right," she said, taking the lead, "we'll go in together, verbally announce our presence, and whoever fails to disperse . . . well . . ." She grinned ruefully. "We'll do what we have to do."

The officers charged en masse, finding exactly what they expected to find within the walls of the dusty tavern. Mayhem.

Melody shouted for the brawlers to desist and to lie down on the floor. Fortunately, three of the men seemed to slowly focus on the officers. They dropped onto the wooden plank floor and were quickly cuffed and escorted to awaiting patrol cars. Three others gave no more notice of law enforcement than they would a gnat buzzing around their heads.

Melody quickly sized up the men, registering the immense size of one of the brawlers. She recognized him from her past dealings at the tavern. She knew he wouldn't go down easily.

Melody turned, making eye contact with Andy Benton and nodding almost imperceptibly toward the giant who was currently pummeling a smaller man with his massive fists. Next, she motioned toward another officer, again nodding at the big man. The officer immediately understood her meaning and acknowledged as much with a crisp nod of his head.

And when Melody gave the signal, the threesome charged, tackling the big man like a collective battering ram and bringing him to the floor with a tremendous thud. Fortunately, he dropped face-first; had he dropped onto his back, they might not have managed to contain him. Each of the two male officers grabbed a huge arm and struggled to subdue him so Melody could cuff him.

She had bent forward to do just that, when suddenly Andy lost his grip on a well-muscled arm. Simultaneously the man bucked like a bull, and his arm rocketed out behind him, his elbow striking Melody in her right eye. The force of the blow launched her backward and into the air. She landed on her back and later recalled having seen stars.

She lay still for a moment, feeling dizzy and disoriented. "Shake it off, Hudson," she told herself, wincing from the pain as she rolled onto her knees and then rose slowly to her feet. Suddenly another officer was at her side and helping her out of the tavern.

A cool burst of evening air helped to enliven her somewhat, and she reached a tentative hand to her eye. Already it had swollen shut, and she knew she would have a shiner soon enough. Since the pain was intense, she hoped she hadn't fractured an orbital bone, as had happened to a fellow officer recently during a similar scene at a different tavern.

"Another day at the office," she quipped when her sergeant appeared at her side, regarding her with concern.

"You need a doctor," he said. He led her to his car and told her to get in.

"My patrol car . . ."

"I'll have someone pick it up and bring it to the hospital," he cut in. "You need medical attention now. Your whole face is bruising, and the swelling is already terrible."

Melody dropped into the passenger seat of his car and reached up to tug the visor down. She saw herself in the mirror and gasped. It wasn't pretty.

Fortunately, an X-ray at the hospital revealed that she hadn't broken any bones in her face, but the doctor told her she'd be black-and-blue for some time after.

"Well, that's something anyway," she had quipped, her hand pressing a pack of ice to her aching face.

Melody insisted to her sergeant that she was fine to drive herself home, and she arrived there after eleven. Her father had already gone to bed, and she felt relieved. Morning was soon enough for her dad to see her badly bruised face.

She considered calling Chase but, due to the late hour, dismissed the idea. She opted for a quick shower rather than a bath, brushed her teeth, and then dropped into bed. She had expected to drift off to sleep quickly, but unfortunately, sleep eluded her again.

She found herself thinking it was definitely time to get off the road and into a different law-enforcement position. Leaving the hospital, after a physician checked out her eye, she had seen the parents of David Lange, the boy who had been injured in the accident the other day and was still in coma. She'd watched his parents moving like robots down a long hallway. Her heart broke for them.

She wondered then, had David Lange received any education about alcohol? Had his parents talked to him? She wondered, would he have benefited from a task force operating in their town? She suspected that, yes, the boy would have benefited. She knew it certainly couldn't have hurt.

She tossed and turned for some time, her face throbbing, and finally she rose from her bed and made her way to the medicine cabinet in the guest bathroom. She pulled out a couple of ibuprofen tablets and swallowed them, then padded back to her room. She closed her good eye and, after twenty minutes or so, finally, finally began to drift off to sleep.

Chapter Nineteen

When Tank wheeled himself into the kitchen the next morning, he found Melody already at the table sipping coffee, the morning paper spread out before her.

"Morning, Pop," she murmured without looking up.

"Mornin'." Tank wheeled himself toward the coffeepot.

"Oh, I'll get it for you, Pop," Melody said, glancing at him and pushing back her chair.

Tank saw her eye then. His eyes widened in horror, and he let out a string of curse words Melody hadn't heard out of his mouth—ever. When he finished his tirade, he wheeled himself to her side, tipping his head back to study her face. "What happened?" he demanded.

"Took an elbow to the eye. No big deal."

He shook his head. "Who did this to you, baby? When I get this cast off, I'm gonna—"

"Pop, you're not going to do anything. This kind of thing comes with the territory. You know that."

Tank shuddered, reaching out to check her facial swelling with a gentle finger. "Ah, Melody, this looks bad. You may have broken a bone. Oh, Lord, I hope not."

She shook her head. "Nope, nothing broken. I'm fine, Pop." She stepped away to get his coffee for him.

"I'm so tired of this doggone chair," he growled. "You don't know how tired I am, Melody." His eyes snared hers, narrowing angrily.

"I do know, Pop," Melody assured him. "But you won't be in it much longer."

She set his coffee mug on the table. Tank didn't pick it up but instead raked an angry hand through his hair. "If I wasn't stuck in this godforsaken chair, I could take care of the sorry excuse for a human being who hurt my daughter," Tank grumbled.

"Pop, I'm fine," she said ruefully. But she understood his anger. It was how she felt toward the boy who had harmed him.

She watched him speculatively, taking in the angry eyes, furrowed brow, and tense lips. Yeah, he was tired of sitting, but there was nothing either of them could do about it—or about the man who had slammed her in the face. Injuries such as hers were par for the course on the job. And, fortunately for the guy who had injured her,

her father was confined to a wheelchair. There was no telling what Tank might have done to him otherwise.

Melody kissed her father on the cheek. "I have to go to work. Love you, Pop."

He looked aghast. "You're not going to work today, are you?"

"I'll be hanging around the station, doing paperwork and taking phone reports until the eye heals." She attempted to sound cheerful, but she hated the idea of being cooped up in the station.

Melody strode to her patrol car and drove to work. She quickly caught up on her paperwork and spent the remainder of the morning manning phones and taking reports. By lunchtime she was bored to tears.

She headed to the staff lunchroom, retrieved her sack lunch from the fridge, and dropped into a chair. Moments later, Manchester and Moore walked into the room.

"Ah, Melody," Manchester said, "you look terrible."

"Awful," Sergeant Moore agreed. "Makes my face hurt just looking at you."

"Yeah, well, you should see the other guy," she quipped.

Moore laughed. "I did. He's in far better shape than you, my friend."

"Did you pass out?" Manchester asked, still wincing after an even closer inspection of her face.

"Nope, but I did see stars."

"I bet you did," her sergeant chimed in. "Are you

feeling all right today? You probably should have taken a day off."

"I have a throbbing headache, and my face hurts," she admitted. "But, otherwise, I'm dandy."

Manchester watched her sympathetically. "Why don't you go home? You look like you could use some rest."

"And an ice bag," her sergeant added.

Melody's lips curved into a grateful smile. "Are you sure you can get by without me? Things are pretty hectic out there today. I've taken two dozen phone reports, and I've followed up on some of the other officers' calls."

"It's about time some of those other officers started pulling their weight," Manchester said fiercely. "There's an obvious inequity in the distribution of call responses out there lately."

Melody glanced up in surprise, her good eye widening and her mouth practically dropping open. She hadn't suspected that her superiors realized just how inequitable the distribution of calls could be, courtesy of a couple of slackers on the force.

"Yes, Melody, we're well aware that you take on the bulk of the call load during your shift," Manchester said in response to her raised eyebrows. "It's part of the reason we think you're the right person to take on the job as coordinator of the DUI and Traffic Safety Task Force. We need a self-starter in the position—a mover and a shaker—and we believe you're that person."

"You know, I've been thinking a lot about the job, but I'm concerned. I need to be busy, and I don't think I'd fare well sitting behind a desk."

"You wouldn't spend much time behind a desk," Manchester assured her. "In fact, there'll be quite a lot of travel to nearby communities and very little sitting, actually," he added. "Not much downtime, actually."

Melody sank back in her seat. Should she take the position? Should she give up her job as patrol officer and try something different within the department? Indeed, she was proud of her work ethic, instilled in her by her hardworking father and mother, and she knew if she took the position, she would move mountains to insure that the task force was a successful departmental venture, but . . . What if she hated the job? What if she missed being out on the road?

"Commander," Melody began tentatively, "if I take the job, and it turns out I'm unhappy, what recourse do I have?"

"We're asking for a minimum eighteen-month commitment, since that should allow enough time to get the program up and running. If you're unhappy at that point, then certainly you can request to go back to the road or put in for a specialized unit."

Her sergeant spoke up then. "Melody, we understand that this position equates to something very different from what you're accustomed to. We also understand that you're comfortable where you are, but we believe you have the smarts and the wherewithal to move up through the ranks here. Accepting this position is a means to showcase your leadership skills. It can only lead to bigger and better things for you in the department."

"What do you think?" Commander Manchester prompted.

Melody glanced from her commander to her sergeant. She could see in their eyes how hopeful they were that she would accept the position, and she felt tremendously flattered. Maybe it was time to try something different. Perhaps having responded to the accident two days before, seeing four kids badly broken as a result of alcohol consumption, had colored her thinking. Or maybe having been injured herself, courtesy of a drunken man in a barroom brawl, had prompted a change of heart. Either way, she realized, she was finally ready to make a change.

"I'd like to accept the position," she said, a smile spreading across her face. She touched her injured eye tentatively. "Maybe it's time I made a change."

Both her sergeant and commander grinned widely, seeming relieved to have persuaded her to step into a new role at the Trentonburg Police Department. And she had to admit, she suddenly felt eager, enlivened, and ready to tackle a new challenge.

Melody arrived at home and found her father and Lucy in the kitchen eating lunch. Lucy gasped at the sight of her injured face, rising from the table and hurrying to wrap her in a hug. "Oh, Melody," she cried, "your father told me what happened. Oh, honey, let me get an ice bag for you."

When Lucy gave it to her, Melody smiled and, to her surprise, felt grateful for the mothering. There were times she missed her mother terribly, usually when she needed her wisdom in some decision-making process. Her mother had always been the cool head in the family, the voice of reason.

"I'm going to change out of these clothes and take a nap," she told them.

"Upstairs?" Lucy asked. "If you'd rather, I can make a bed for you on the couch."

"I think I'll head out to my place," she said. She had been spending her days there anyway and preferred the comfortable mattress in the tiny bedroom to the larger bed in the room upstairs.

"Are you sure?" Tank asked, frowning.

"Yeah, the truth is, I want to be in my own bed."

"We understand," Lucy said. "If you need anything, pick up the phone, and I can be there in the blink of an eye."

Melody headed upstairs and changed into cozy sweats. She stepped into the kitchen briefly. "I'll see you both later."

"Oh, honey," Lucy said, "I'll bet you could use these." She passed her a couple of ibuprofen tablets along with a glass of water.

Melody smiled her thanks and swallowed the pills. She gave Lucy a quick hug and then headed for her cozy bed.

Inside her little house, she realized she should call Chase. But for reasons she couldn't fathom, she didn't make the call. . . .

Chase tried to reach Melody at work shortly after school let out, but to no avail. He tried her cell phone but got her voice mail. He scowled, a feeling of alarm settling over him.

He made a quick decision to duck out of a meeting, advising Jill to explain that he was called away on an important matter, and then he drove to Melody's house. He spotted Tank and his aunt sitting on the front porch, enjoying the sunshine that peeked through fluffy white clouds.

He parked and strode over to them, lifting a hand in greeting.

"Hello, Chase," Tank said.

"How are you, Chase?" Lucy asked.

"Fine. Fine. Hey, have either of you talked to Melody today? I've tried to reach her, but I haven't managed to get a hold of her."

"She's resting," Tank said.

Lucy nodded. "I think she's in more pain than she's letting on."

Chase's eyes widened fearfully. "What do you mean, Melody's in pain?"

"You don't know . . . ?" Lucy asked, eyes widening as she turned to Tank.

"Chase, Melody's going to be just fine, but she was injured last night breaking up a barroom brawl," Tank said.

"What?" Chase exclaimed, raking a rough hand through his hair. "Why didn't she call me? Why didn't you call me?"

"I didn't know myself until this morning, son," Tank said.

"Where is she? I need to see her."

"Honey," Lucy said soothingly, "she's sleeping now, and I think we should let her rest."

Chase scrubbed a hand over his jaw, seeming to consider whether to let her sleep or not. "I need to see her. Please." His voice was husky with emotion.

"She's at the little house," Tank said, indicating the tiny cottage with a nod. "If she's asleep, will you try not to wake her?"

"Uh, yeah," Chase said, already striding away.

He tapped lightly on the door when he arrived, but when Melody didn't call out for him to enter, he quietly pushed the door open and stepped inside. He crossed the tiny living room and stepped into the bedroom. He found Melody sleeping on her left side, her light covers tossed off of her and lying on the floor.

He stepped closer and winced when he spied her horribly swollen face and eye. "Oh, Melody," he murmured, reaching out to tenderly stroke her cheek. She stirred but didn't wake up. He wanted desperately to talk to her, to hold her, to hear from her own lips that she was okay. But it would have to wait. Clearly she was exhausted. He lifted her covers off the floor and carefully draped them over her, tucking them around her.

As much as he wanted to lie down beside her and hold her in his arms, he dropped instead into the chair beside the bed, tipping his head back and breathing deeply to slow his pounding heart. When Tank said Melody had been injured, he had thought he might die from the shock of it.

Why hadn't she called him last night? Why hadn't she called him today?

He took a deep, steadying breath. When Melody woke up, he needed to be calm and collected. But his efforts at calming himself were futile—he wasn't accustomed to this feeling of helplessness. He was a take-charge guy, physically strong, and used to making things happen. He wanted to protect Melody. But . . . she didn't need his protection—wouldn't want his protection. She was strong and capable. She was fine. Her face would heal. He silently repeated the words like a mantra, willing them to be true.

When she finally woke up, her eyes fluttering open and lighting on Chase's face, she sat up and pushed the covers back. She yawned, meeting his gaze and smiling tentatively into his eyes. "Hi," she said.

Chase sat on the bed beside her and pulled her into

his arms, careful to avoid further injuring her face. "Melody, why didn't you call me?" he asked softly. "I just found out you'd been injured when I stopped by to see you."

"I got in really late last night. I didn't want to wake you."

"Why didn't you call me at work today?"

Melody shrugged, and Chase stood abruptly, paced the tiny room, and then returned to her bedside. "You thought I'd be angry, seeing you injured," he said, watching her eyes in an attempt to read her. He shook his head, confused. "You didn't trust me to handle seeing you injured."

"I actually didn't think about that, Chase," she said in her defense, but a tiny voice in the back of her mind told her that Chase's words were true. She'd feared he would react the way her father had, with anger and a bent toward revenge, and she hadn't wanted to deal with that.

"Melody, you should have called me. I should have been the first person you called."

"But, Chase . . ."

He shook his head and raked a hand through his hair. "Melody, you have to trust that I'll be there for you. I know you think I can't, or ultimately won't, be able to handle your job, but you have to give me the opportunity to prove to you that I can. We can't think in terms of a future together if you're unwilling to trust me," he said in an agonized voice.

Melody swung her legs over the side of the bed, and her anguished eyes connected with his. "But what if you can't? What if you decide it's too much, and you leave? I see it all the time at work. In my line of work, relationships fail all . . . the . . . time, Chase."

"And law enforcement relationships work all the time too. Look at your folks," he pointed out.

She shook her head. "It was hard on my mom, Chase. So hard. I watched her, Chase. I watched her so many nights when Pop was late getting home, sitting in her chair, staring at the phone as if willing it to ring."

"Melody, I understand what I'm in for. Okay? It's worth it. You're worth it." Chase took a deep, steadying breath, his eyes lighting on her injury. "Oh, Melody, it's bad. Who did this to you? Tell me."

Melody rose and found herself unsteady on her feet. "There," she said in an accusatory tone. "You think you have to protect me, defend me against the big, bad guy who did this to me. Well, Chase, you don't—and neither does my father."

Chase watched Melody, mouth agape. "If I were standing in front of you with a black eye and a badly bruised face, don't tell me you . . ."

"Okay, yeah, I'd be angry. I'd want to . . ."

"What?"

"Give whomever a dose of his own medicine, I guess."

"Okay, so you know, I'm not going after the guy, Melody, because presumably he's behind bars, but that doesn't mean I don't want to. I'd like to, all right—but I won't."

Melody sat on the chair beside her bed, and Chase dropped onto mattress. "Honey, you have to trust me. You have to understand that a part of me wants to protect you. It's only natural."

"You want me to quit my job," she accused.

Chase rose and paced again. "No, I do not. I understand I don't have that right."

"But isn't there a part of you that would like to see me out of law enforcement and in something more safe and sedate?" she pressed.

"Okay, yeah, the truth is, yeah. I'd like you in a job where I wouldn't have to worry about you every day, but you know what? That's not my decision to make, is it?"

"No."

Melody felt hot tears spring to her eyes. She needed to think. She needed to sleep. Her face throbbed, and she didn't feel like talking now. She loved Chase, but could she count on him to stand beside her, to be supportive of her career decisions? She studied his face, told herself she saw indecision there. "You can't handle this. . . ." she murmured aloud, not realizing she'd spoken the words until Chase shook his head confusedly.

"Melody, I can. Honey, you're projecting your fears onto me. You're not giving me enough credit."

Melody ran a hand through her hair, wincing when she inadvertently touched her bruised cheek. "Chase,

I need time to think. I'm just so tired." She watched him through agonized eyes. "Will you go, please?"

"May I call you later?" he implored.

Melody didn't miss the anguish on his face. She realized she was pushing him away, but then, that had always been her modus operandi, she realized. Her father was right. She pushed people away when things got too serious. What did that say about her?

Chase took a tentative step toward her, reaching out to tenderly stroke her cheek. "Don't push me away, Mel. Please."

"Give me time. . . ."

"Okay," he said crisply, "if that's what you really want." With that, he strode out of the small house.

Chapter Twenty

During the weeks that followed her injury, Melody was grateful she had a new job to occupy her time and her mind. To her surprise, Commander Manchester had formally pulled her off the road the day after she accepted the position. He had advised her to telephone task force coordinators in other communities about their successes and failures as they had embarked upon creating the new units within their own departments.

Melody found herself pleasantly surprised to learn of the successes many of the task forces boasted on the community-education front. One claimed to have reduced the number of DUIs within their community by thirty percent. Melody viewed that discovery as a challenge—she would be sure that her community

246

registered an even greater reduction in alcohol-related incidents.

Long days at the office fast became Melody's norm, even more so than before. She just didn't want to go home, where, during her quiet times, she couldn't help but think about Chase. He had tried to reach her often during the week after she pushed him away, but she hadn't taken his calls. Her thoughts were just too tumultuous at that point, and she truly wasn't sure what she could say to him if she did speak to him. She knew she had been wrong to chase him away, but she simply didn't know how to fix things—or even if she wanted to. What *did* she want?

She had to admit, she felt miserable without him, but she could acknowledge now that she had essentially shut down after her injury—perhaps because it had been only one of many on-the-job injuries that had plagued her in recent years. Perhaps she had begun to comprehend her own mortality, realizing that a well-placed blow from the man in the bar could have actually killed her, had he struck her in the temple. The shot to her eye was bad enough.

She couldn't be certain what had prompted her actions that afternoon Chase stopped by her little house, but she felt terrible for them. Chase had only wanted to be there for her, to comfort her. She knew that. He had accused her of projecting her fears onto him, and she had. But her fears were well-founded; she knew that. She had seen too many law enforcement relationships fail.

She remembered accusing Chase of wanting her out of her job. The irony was, she had taken a new position, which, arguably, wasn't nearly as dangerous as her previous job had been. She'd accused him of an inability to handle a job she wasn't even in any longer. It was a sad state of affairs, she acknowledged to herself.

On one positive note, to her surprise, she loved her new job. Unfortunately, she couldn't even share that news with the man she loved. She just couldn't bring herself to pick up the phone and call him.

As was usual, her work became her focus, her passion, and she knew that, with her at the helm, the task force would be a success. She would settle for nothing less.

When she arrived home late Friday evening, she found her father and Lucy at the kitchen table.

"I've kept your dinner warm," Lucy told her.

Melody smiled at the woman who had become a dear friend to her and who had earned her admiration. Lucy clearly loved her gruff father, devoting herself to his care. Melody couldn't help but love her for that.

"I appreciate that," Melody told Lucy, smiling warmly. "I'm famished."

"Did you eat lunch, honey? You're looking awfully thin," her father observed.

"I grabbed something from the vending machine at work," Melody told him absently. "If you both don't mind, I'm going to run upstairs really quick and change out of this uniform."

Dressed in cozy sweats, she was back in a flash and sat down to a plate of meatloaf and mashed potatoes. The delicious comfort food went a long way toward lifting her spirits.

"Yum, this is heaven," she said, closing her eyes and savoring the taste as Lucy beamed at the compliment.

"How was your day, Melody?" she asked.

"Busy. There's so much to get done to get this task force off the ground."

"Such as?" her father prompted.

"Well," she said between bites of mashed potato, "I'm going to open up the unit to the community."

"Anybody can join?" Lucy asked with interest.

Melody nodded.

"How are you going to rally support?" Tank inquired.

"I'm sending out a press release Monday, and I'll be recording a radio spot Wednesday. The sooner I get people on board, the sooner we'll start seeing changes in our community. I talked to a task force coordinator over in Lewistown, and he suggested that the more people you get involved, the more resources you'll find available to you. Frankly, everybody has a stake in the issue of drunk driving and other alcohol-related crimes. We all pay a high price for them," Melody said.

Tank nodded, thrilled to see the enthusiasm on his daughter's face. Most of the time lately she moped around as if she'd lost the love of her life, which, he suspected, she had. That reality prompted him to broach the subject of Chase.

"Uh, Melody," he began somewhat tentatively, "did you call Chase back? He called again yesterday."

Melody's gaze jerked up from her plate of food, and Tank grimaced when he saw the flash of pain in her eyes, realizing he'd put it there. She shook her head but didn't speak.

"It's time you talked to him, if you ask me."

"I'm not asking you, Pop," Melody said pointedly.

"Honey, Ed says poor old Chase is beside himself with grief, half the time moping around like a lovesick kid and the other half, ill-tempered as a hungry bear. Ed says when he isn't working, he's at his property, attacking the house as if its completion might save his very soul."

"He's not my problem," Melody muttered. "I'm not his problem," she added.

"No? If he's not your problem, then whose problem is he?" Tank muttered. "He's lovesick over you, girl, and you're lovesick over him. Honey, go talk to him. Make things right."

"I . . . I don't know how," she murmured miserably. "I've really messed things up, I think."

"You don't know that for sure. Besides, it doesn't matter who did what," Tank said fiercely. "Just fix it."

Lucy patted Melody's hand. "Melody, talk to Chase."

Melody had confided in Lucy after she'd practically

forced Chase out of her life, and Lucy had urged her to give him a chance to understand her fears. But that was a difficult thing to do, since she wasn't sure how to voice her fears—or, specifically, what they were, exactly.

"I'll . . . consider calling him," Melody said.

"Well, that's something anyway," Tank groused.

Chase stepped onto his folks' porch, dropped onto a bench, and tugged his muddied boots off his feet. He entered the house, shrugging out of his jacket, and then headed for the kitchen, intent on making himself a sandwich as a late dinner.

He was surprised to find his parents at the table, sipping lemonade. "Hello," he greeted them, watching them warily, since they both gave him disgusted stares.

"What'd I do?" he griped as he reached into the fridge and pulled out luncheon meat, cheese, and condiments.

"It's not what you did, son, it's what you didn't do," his mother told him.

"And what's that?" he said irritably as he reached for a loaf of bread. He didn't want to have this conversation, since he suspected he knew where it might be leading.

"You know very well what you didn't do, son," Mary chortled. "What you haven't done. You haven't gone over to Melody's to talk to her."

"She won't talk to me," he said pointedly.

"Try again," Ed urged.

"Honey, maybe she's ready to talk now," Mary said encouragingly. "Lucy tells me she thinks Mel might be ready to talk."

"Yeah, well, I tried to talk to her. She accused me of having a problem with her job, when the truth is, she wanted to run me off all along. Turns out, she's the commitment-phobe around here."

"Do you have a problem with Melody's job, son?" Ed asked in measured tones.

"No . . . well, yeah, on some level. I mean, who wouldn't? The woman carries a .45 caliber pistol and comes homes from work bruised and swollen from breaking up barroom brawls." He turned to his father. "Sound appealing to you, Pop? You think you'd be patient if Mom was a gun-toting law woman who rarely even made it home on time from work each night?"

Ed looked puzzled. "Who would cook my dinner?"

"Okay, there you go!" Chase said, grateful for even a small victory.

Mary glared at her husband. "If I were a law woman, you would love me and support me and cook dinner for me when I got home late, since that's what two people who love each other do," she said, daring her husband to argue.

He didn't. "Oh, okay, honey. You're right. That's what I would do."

"Oh, you would not," Chase muttered, rubbing his hands over his eyes. "But you know what? That's exactly what I intended to do. I was more than prepared to do whatever it took to make a relationship with Melody work. I love the woman. Heck, I was going to propose. . . ."

"You were?" Mary cried eagerly. "Oh, Chase, that's wonderful."

"She won't speak to me, Ma. I can't very well propose if she won't even talk to me."

"Try again, Chase," his mother urged. "Melody needs you."

"Right!" he said dubiously. "The truth is, she doesn't *need* anybody. She can handle herself just fine, thank you very much."

"Chase, son, it'll be all right. You and Melody will work things out," Ed said.

Would Melody talk to him? He doubted it. He hadn't even seen her once during the last couple of weeks, and that was a curious thing. Usually he saw her several times each week, when she responded to calls at the high school.

"Dad, the woman won't even take calls at the high school," he said angrily.

"What's that supposed to mean?" Mary demanded hotly. "That Melody's avoiding calls to avoid seeing you? You know better than that. She would no more shirk her responsibilities than—"

"I call 'em like I see 'em," Chase cut in, quickly assembling a sandwich and shoving the ingredients back into the fridge. "But you're right, she wouldn't shirk her responsibilities, but she can sure shirk me." He shook his head confusedly. What had he just said?

"Melody's the bravest young woman we know." Ed spoke up. "She would not shirk her responsibilities to avoid contact with you."

Chase shrugged and dropped into a chair to eat his sandwich. He bit in hard, chewing angrily, as if taking out his frustrations on the sandwich.

"Go talk to her, boy," Ed said. "If you don't try to work things out, you're liable to lose the love of your life."

Chase scrubbed a hand over his stubbled jaw, then snared his father's gaze. "Have you seen her? How's her eye?"

"She's looking better," Ed said. "Still swollen and bruised, but better." Ed eyed him speculatively. "You going to talk to her, son?"

"I . . . I don't know yet."

Chase spent the better part of the next day working on his house. He'd accomplished a good deal over the past several weeks. All the framing was done, the wiring and plumbing were completed, and all the walls had been drywalled. It wouldn't be long before he could move in.

It was now late afternoon, and Chase stood back to assess the home's front facade. Though it resembled an old-time farmhouse, the home boasted every modern amenity inside. He loved the wide porch that wrapped around the front and along one side and to the back. He envisioned cool summer evenings rocking on that porch, either in back, overlooking the beautiful mountain peak, or in front, overlooking the lovely green pasture. In his mind's eye he saw Melody in a chair beside him, but, to his horror, the picture image evaporated like a cloud of smoke.

He missed her desperately. He remembered his conversation with his parents the evening before. They wanted him to talk to Melody, and he had made repeated attempts to reach her by phone—to no avail. If only he could get through to her. He hadn't stopped by her dad's house, however, and he wondered if she would agree to talk to him if he did.

Would she give him another chance? He had to talk to her, try to make her see that she could trust him to remain by her side, in spite of whatever trials came their way.

He turned his gaze back to the house. Suddenly a burst of sunlight filtered through the clouds, the bright light providing a stunning backdrop to the farmhouse. The scene was beautiful, like a painting, and he hoped it might be a hopeful sign that Melody would see clear to taking him back into her life.

Chase drove home, showered, changed into jeans and a T-shirt, and headed to Melody's house. Moments later, when he parked, he was surprised to see her stepping out the front door. She spotted him, and he watched her lay what appeared to be a package and something else he couldn't identify on a small table near the door.

He climbed out of the car and approached her tentatively, standing at the base of the steps and surveying her lovely face. He was relieved to see that his father had been right about her eye looking better. He noticed she was dressed in a floral print sundress that accentuated her deep blue eyes. Even with her black eye, she was beautiful.

Melody hesitantly met his gaze. "Hello, Chase."

"Hello, Melody."

She noticed that he studied her face, seemingly relieved to see her eye much improved.

"You look good," he told her.

"Thanks."

"Can we talk?"

"I was . . . actually just on my way to talk to you," Melody told him. "On the porch?" she suggested, unaware that Tank and Lucy had heard Chase drive up and were listening to the couple unabashedly from behind a curtain in the open living room window.

Chase sat down on the porch swing. He leaned forward and clasped his hands together, watching Melody intently as she retrieved a chair and sat down.

"Chase, I owe you an apology. A big apology," she said with a tremulous laugh.

Chase still sat quietly, his brown eyes fixed on her face.

She took his silence as a cue to continue. "Chase,

I . . ." She swallowed nervously. "When you came by my house that day and saw my face, you were right when you accused me of not trusting you enough to call you to tell you I'd been hurt."

"How did you think I would react, Melody?" he asked her softly. "I mean, surely you knew I'd be upset at seeing you injured but that I would be able to handle it."

"But I didn't know if you could handle it," she practically moaned.

"You didn't give me a chance."

Melody made lingering eye contact. "I . . . I know, and you had every right to be upset. If you had been injured, I would have been equally upset."

"What'd they say?" Tank whispered loudly. "I can't hear them very well."

"Shh," Lucy said, "they'll hear you."

Melody watched Chase expectantly, her heart suddenly beating an awkward rhythm in her chest. She noted that dark circles framed his lower eyelids, and she suspected that, like her, he wasn't sleeping well.

Did he miss her as much as she missed him? she wondered. She pushed the thought aside. Of course not. She had hurt him deeply by pushing him away. Could he ever forgive her?

"Chase, I'm so sorry. If I could go back in time and change that day—the day I pushed you away—I would," she said with anguish. "I'm still trying to fully understand why I did it."

"You accused me of wanting you to quit your job," Chase reminded her softly, straightening on the swing to await her response.

"I know. You see, I've seen it so many times with my co-workers. Relationships end, marriages break up, because of the stress and worry—or conflicts over the long hours. So many things . . . And you've made comments about my job in the past . . . Being married to a police officer is hard, Chase. I guess a part of me believed that if we made a commitment to each other, you would naturally be threatened by my work— eventually anyway—so threatened you would leave, so I think . . ."

"You pushed me away before I could hurt you by leaving!" Chase said, understanding dawning. "Melody, I would never leave you." He crossed the distance between them, kneeling in front of her. "I would never hurt you that way." He laced a hand through her hair. "You have to believe me. I understand now."

"Well, I'm glad you understand," Melody said tremulously, "because I'm not certain I completely understand myself."

"Look, Melody, on some level I guess I am threatened by your job. As I told you that day at your house, it's only natural, but I would never presume to tell you to quit a job you love. You wouldn't be happy in another line of work. I know that. And, Melody, you have to know I'm proud of you. You're an . . . an amazing woman! There's no other way to say it."

Melody smiled but then sobered. "Chase, do you remember when I responded to a call at the school one time, and you asked me if I'd ever considered another line of work? That really worried me."

Chase appeared to search his memory. "You're right, I did ask that. But, honey, I wasn't asking because I had some notion you would quit your job for me. I guess I was trying to gauge how you felt about having children. But I realized it was kind of early to ask such a personal question."

Melody considered his explanation. So Chase had been attempting to find out how she felt about having kids?

"Do you want kids, Chase?" Melody asked, bracing herself for his answer. She wanted children. Had always wanted children.

"I do!" he said quickly. "I always have."

"Me too!"

"Good, that's good," Tank said happily from the living room, snaring Lucy's gaze. "I want grandkids! Soon!"

"Tank!" Lucy scolded. "Keep quiet. This isn't about what you want."

Tank gave Lucy a startled glance but clamped his mouth shut.

Chase reached for Melody's hand. He turned her hand over, kissing her palm and causing her heart to give an erratic thump. "I've missed you," he said softly.

"I've missed you too."

"Is he proposing to her?" Tank asked excitedly. "He's on bended knee. Lord knows, I hope he's proposing."

"He's not proposing yet," Lucy said, waving at him to be quiet. "Give them a minute, Tank."

Melody rose from her chair, and Chase stood up. He smiled into her eyes and then pulled her into an embrace.

Melody pulled back slightly. "Do you forgive me, Chase? Can we start over?"

He nuzzled his cheek against her face. "You're in my arms, aren't you?"

"You're in his arms, aren't you!" Tank whispered excitedly.

"Tank, quiet!" Lucy said in an exasperated tone.

Tank turned to Lucy, grinned, and to her surprise, pulled her onto his lap and into his arms. "And now you're in my arms, Lucy," he said gleefully. "Right where you belong."

Lucy smiled into his eyes, kissed him gently on the lips, and then turned her attention back to Chase and Melody, listening.

Melody stepped away from Chase with a smile and reached for the rosebush and box of chocolates she'd put on a nearby table. She passed them to him, and he smiled. "Just what I always wanted, chocolates and a plant with a root-ball." He laughed.

"Ah, Melody!" Tank cried loudly then. "Not a plant with a root-ball! No guy wants a plant with a root-ball!"

"Tank! Hush now!" Lucy scolded, but then she burst out laughing.

Both Chase and Melody turned toward the window. "Tank, Lucy, we know you're there," they said in unison.

"Melody, you gave Chase a plant with a root-ball?" Tank shouted. "Melody, I taught you better than that. No man likes a plant with a root system. It means you expect us to plant something, and nine times out of ten we don't want anything to do with digging a hole. Men like cut flowers, for Pete's sake. Something we can toss into the garbage can when they wilt, or out the car window."

"Pop!" Melody called, her voice alight with laughter. "If I start giving you cut flowers for your birthday, you'll have no one but yourself to blame."

"Besides, Tank," Chase said sternly, "I'm thrilled with my plant. I'm going to plant it at our home—the one I'll be sharing with Melody," he added, smiling hopefully and lovingly into her eyes. "Will you marry me?" he whispered.

Melody stepped into his embrace again, and she realized she'd found home in his arms. "I love you," she whispered back. "And yes, of course I'll marry you."

"What'd you say?" Tank demanded, and he turned to Lucy. "What'd they say? Speak up, both of you. We can't hear you!"

"I was just telling Melody that if she arrives home from work late at night, and she will," Chase added ruefully, "I'll have dinner waiting. And I'll be ever supportive of her job as patrol officer and never, ever give her grief about it."

"Well, as it happens, I'm no longer a patrol officer," Melody said, her face alight with humor. "I quit that particular job. But I have started a new one . . ."